Crazy Bastard

Trapped in Haunted Whorehouse

Danny Salazar

CRAZY BASTARD TRAPPED IN HAUNTED WHOREHOUSE

iUniverse books may be ordered through booksellers or by contacting:

iUniverse
1663 Liberty Drive
Bloomington, IN 47403
www.iuniverse.com
844-349-9409

ISBN: 978-1-6632-4170-2 (sc)
ISBN: 978-1-6632-4203-7 (hc)
ISBN: 978-1-6632-4169-6 (e)

Library of Congress Control Number: 2022911996

Print information available on the last page.

iUniverse rev. date: 08/25/2022

CHAPTER 1

Skank Hill, Nevada

April 23, 1865
Two weeks after the end of the Civil War

Skank Hill was a small, rugged town, established as a new community in Nevada. Hundreds of travelers from all over the country couldn't have been happier as they settled into life after a long journey of riding on their stiff wooden wagons. The town was still new and growing and didn't have many businesses yet—only a Chinese pig farm run by Irish immigrants; a tarot card–reading service belonging to an ex-slave owner (she was addicted to opium and ate roadkill); a homosexual jailer who kept the town in check with his homosexual ways; and the last place at the far end of the road, a bright-white plantation home known as the town's saloon whorehouse, called the White Man's Tuna Twat Palace.

The Irish guy who ran the whorehouse, should have been running the pig farm. It was paradise to the new settlers, but that didn't last long since two drunken morons were plastered at the gambling table in the middle of the whorehouse playing Three-Card Monte. Clayton and Flynn were their names, two bank-robbing brothers who started trouble wherever they went. They were well known as the Dodge City Villains, two rotten criminals from Kansas, but karma played against them this time.

"Do you hear all those newcomers outside making this town their new home, Flynn? Everybody thinks just because a town has just been established as part of this country that they can claim any piece of land they want!" Clayton said.

"We did the same thing, baby brother, so let's not be hypocrites," Flynn whispered, hoping Clayton wouldn't make another horrible scene in front of everyone, like he had done many times before.

"Shut the fuck up, Flynn. I don't think anybody here asked you for your goddamn opinion!"

Flynn didn't want to respond; he knew it would cause nothing but drama in public, and he didn't want every eye in the whorehouse staring at them. It was already bad enough that they were wanted, dead or alive, in almost every state. Drawing attention to themselves could go wrong. He ignored his brother's rude behavior and continued playing cards without even thinking about it.

The whorehouse was packed that day. The drifters and the travelers kept piling in to see the amazing White Man's Tuna Twat Palace. Their colorful grand opening decorations made the place look fantastic. Every beautiful whore at the palace was working on every floor to please as many customers as possible.

After about an hour of playing cards, the brothers' cheap Overholt whiskey bottle was almost empty, and Clayton was thirsty for more. "Hey! Pretty lady, do you think you can take your ass behind the bar and fetch me another bottle of this shit? We've been here longer than most people, and I think it's fair to say that we should get served first, before everybody else." He hammered his fist on top of the table.

Although it was a whorehouse, their crazed-out waitress, who came to work looking like a train wreck because she was badly hungover from the night before, wasn't going to deal with anyone's shit that night. She made sure to lay that on Clayton, being as strict as she needed to be. "Look here, you big-lipped fucking monkey. My pussy may be wet, but I'm not trying to fuck with you right now! You'd better not rush me again, or I will steal your horse and make your mama suck its big-horse fucking dick, just like the good old days." Everybody in the whorehouse overheard her as she stuck it to Clayton; she trying her best to make him feel salty for his rude behavior.

But the mean and drunken Clayton wasn't feeling salty at all. His face was bright red, and he shot steam right back at her. "Look here, bitch! This is a fucking whorehouse, so you'd better start acting like one, or I will go over to your mama's house and make one out of her!"

Flynn couldn't believe that his brother was causing a scene again. Like any other good brother would have done, he tried to help Clayton calm down in any way possible so that, hopefully, the rest of their night would go smoothly—benefitting themselves but mainly everybody there. But as much as Flynn wanted everything to go perfectly right, it was far too late for that.

Many people were at the whorehouse at that moment, but one particular gentleman in the crowd recognized their voices from across the room—Sheriff Benson. Benson was a lawman out of Dodge City, Kansas, and he knew all about Clayton and Flynn, back when they caused all kinds of mischief. Now, as he sat in his chair at a poker table, trying his best to enjoy his visit to this new town of Skank Hill, Nevada, he was left with no choice but to rise slowly from his seat and walk over to their table to take them both into custody. Normally, he would have avoided the entire situation, but the brothers' criminal reputation had preceded them, and the rewards on the wanted posters could make Sheriff Benson a rich man; that made it almost impossible to turn his back on them.

"Looks like I got you two boys now, and don't even try to move because I have a loaded revolver pointed right at your backs. If you try to run, I will open fire with this motherfucker and allow everybody to witness your brains splatter all over your laps. Let's not make this too difficult, gentlemen. When I ask you to stand on your feet, start heading out that front door so I can hog-tie both of your asses to my wagon. It's going to be a long trip back to Dodge City, boys; let's start moving out now!"

Sheriff Benson should have known that Clayton and Flynn were not going to go out that easily. As they rose from their seats and headed toward the front door, Clayton began to speak as if it was his last words on earth. "Please, Sheriff, we don't need to go through all of this. My brother and I haven't been in trouble with the law for years. We came to Skank Hill to start our lives over again so we can finally learn how to be good men, like every child of God should be."

Sheriff Benson didn't want to hear any of their excuses, and he continued to direct them toward the front entrance. "I don't feel sorry for no convict's, boy, and I sure as hell ain't going to start today with your stupid asses! The only thing I feel sorry about is your poor, worthless, bitch mother, who must face the fact that her two fucked-up sons are nothing but a waste of breath on this earth and need to be publicly hanged so the whole town can see your little chicken necks snap like tree twigs!"

It almost seemed like it was over for the two outlaw brothers, but God must have been on their side. With Sheriff Benson feeling sure that he had Clayton and Flynn right where he wanted them, he suddenly made the biggest mistake of his law enforcement career. He did the one thing that no officer of the law should in the line of duty—he turned his back on his captured prisoners without searching them first. Sheriff Benson wasn't always the brightest man. Because of that, he was too stupid to know that Flynn was working his way behind him with a revolver in hand—and it didn't help that Benson was distracted by hearing Clayton's bullshit drunken stories of why he should let them go.

"Please! Sheriff Benson, don't take us back to those dreadful jail cells. My beloved dead wife is waiting for me, hanging by her neck on a barbed wire rope back at home. She would have been worried about me if I didn't make it home on time. I think it would be mighty kind of you to let me go, Sheriff, so that I can be back in her dead arms again and in her dead, dry pussy."

Sheriff Benson ignored Clayton's drunken, nutty behavior and continued to tie him up. "Oh, Clayton, you sure are a funny piece of shit! I might just have to leave you two boys here with the queer-bait jailers and let them have their way with you two." Suddenly, Sheriff Benson realized that Flynn was out of sight and had no idea where he had gone. "Hey! Where the fuck did he go?"

Benson was quickly startled by the sounds of a chamber spinning in a revolver, right behind. "Don't move, Sheriff, or you're good as dead! Let my brother go, and nobody will get killed!"

Sheriff Benson was a proud law enforcement man who always held his head high when on his job and would never let his team down for anything, "Fuck your fucking brother and your fucking mother too! I'm a goddamn sheriff, and I will do whatever the fuck I want, even if that means fucking your brother in his ass and making your mother watch!

I bet she would enjoy seeing her son getting fucked in his ass while she fingers herself with a rusty fucking pitchfork!"

This was a tough situation to avoid, but, like in every town or city worldwide, there was always one good-hearted citizen trying to step in to do the right thing. Luckily at this very moment in the whorehouse, the White Man's Tuna Twat Palace, that man's name was Michael Pussfry, a small-time peasant out of Texas who did odd jobs around saloons and horse ranches—sometimes sexual but mostly just shoveling shit. He didn't care, just as long as he could follow in the footsteps of his old man, who had recently passed away.

"Hey, there, fellas! Now I know it's none of my business, but is there any way we can just let bygones be bygones and go our separate ways? We are all here today at this charming whorehouse, and I feel it would be best if we just cut the violence, gentlemen, and have a great time."

But neither Benson nor Flynn liked that idea, so they had no choice but to dispose of him at that moment. "Listen here," Flynn shouted. "I have robbed many banks in my lifetime, and we always run into nose-digging motherfuckers like you, and there is only one way I handle them!" Without a second thought, he quickly pointed his revolver at Michael's head and gently pulled the trigger.

Blood flew all over the walls and even struck some of the innocent people in the crowd as they all watched Michael Pussfry's body slowly hit the floor.

"You stupid fuck!" Sheriff Benson shouted. "I'm going to make sure you hang for that!"

Flynn could not have cared less. He quickly looked over at Sheriff Benson and said, "That's one for the bad guys, boys! If you don't step aside, your body will be lying next to his, and I'll do nothing but stand over your dead ass and piss all over your big fucking gorilla head!"

Stupidly, Benson gave his full attention to Clayton as the shot went off; he had forgotten that Flynn was still behind him with a loaded revolver.

"Put your hands in the air, Sheriff. It's all over for you! My brother, Clayton, and I have you caught in a real ugly situation now, so the best thing for you is to surrender your gun and hope for the best. I am your god on earth, boy. I'm the one who says whether you live or die today. You understand me?"

Sheriff Benson knew it would be best to stand his ground and try to shoot his way out of the troubled position he had gotten himself into. But once again, another good-hearted citizen stepped in—but this time, he came with a physical approach that got everyone in the whorehouse involved.

This man was fed up with all three of them and wanted them all to shut up. He took off both of his cowboy boots and threw one at Clayton and the other at Flynn. Then he took his half-full glass of beer and threw it right at the sheriff's head, knocking his favorite cowboy hat onto the floor. "All three of you little whiney bitches can suck my big rhino fucking cock, and so can all your sisters too. Ha-ha-ha!" He gave all three of them a strange look as he dug his hands into his pants to jerk off.

Everyone in the whorehouse quickly felt uncomfortable, with this strange man jerking himself off. They all grew angry because they felt that their good times were being ruined. With anger running through everyone's veins, they all decided to shit on each other, and they turned the entire whorehouse upside down. They turned over tables and knocked over lanterns. All the beautiful new walls decorated with blood, piss, and beer. Everybody was fighting, with no one coming between them.

The only one who was not involved was the British piano player. The suicidal horse thief out of Dartford, England, had been offered a job at the whorehouse by his little sister, who had become a ragged whore and knew about every whorehouse in all thirty-six states. He felt this could be his lucky break from all the drama back at home, and so now he played the piano as he had never played before. It was a damn shame that nobody noticed, but he didn't care. He kept playing and playing as everybody in the whorehouse continued to fight each other.

"Take this, you motherfuckers!" yelled a one-legged Confederate veteran from back in the corner, holding an enormous stick of dynamite.

The short fuse on the stick didn't give the crowd enough time to make a run for it. Before anyone could say a word, the blast went off, killing everybody there. There were no more beers and pussy, no more shouting and fighting, and no more piano man playing the music. Everyone who had attended the whorehouse that day was dead. It wasn't the best way to start an up-and-coming town, but as with most towns back in those days, they just cleaned up the mess and pretended it never happened.

New owners would come along and try to build and fix it again, but they never lasted longer than a week—they either ended up dead or in a mental hospital. After many years, they decided to close it up for good because of all the evil caused.

Now, it sits there waiting, until one day—maybe—another desperate owner will come along and make it come alive again.

CHAPTER 2

One Hundred Thirteen Years Later

1978

A new life was beginning for a family of three as they cruised down the highway in their green Ford Pinto after leaving their shabby home in McAllen, Texas. They were headed for Nevada, hoping to strike it rich in Las Vegas. The single father and his two high school dropout daughters had no choice but to leave home to seek their fortune because there was no work in McAllen. Most people from that town headed to the Midwest to find work in the new steel mill, but this family refused to do that.

The father, Johnny Lee Cherry, was a Vietnam veteran who had done nothing since the war but fixing cars and shooting heroin. He hoped that one day he could reunite with his lovely wife, who had been dead for almost ten years, after a wood-chipper accident. His daughters were never the same after witnessing her horrible death.

Taryn was his older daughter, and Nicole was the younger. Without a mother to teach them proper ladylike ways, they learned from their junkie father and every hooker he brought home. Johnny was nowhere near father of the year, but he tried his best to make his two lovely daughters as happy as they could be. Even though they were both going down the wrong road in life, they still felt that the only way their family could survive was by sticking together and allowing no one to tear them apart.

"I sure can't wait until we get to Vegas, Dad," Nicole said. "It's going to be so exciting to see all the wonderful lights shining so bright at night, and I just know it's going to be so fucking easy to score dope out there. I bet they got class-A Colombian coke! What do you think, Dad?"

Johnny didn't care to get involved in his daughter's crazy activities because he firmly believed they were no longer little girls and were old enough to make their own decisions. "Oh, sweetheart, you have grown up so quickly. I can't believe where the years have gone. If only your mother were alive, things would be so different."

Nicole refused to let her dad be stuck in the past. "You must move on from the past, old man! The fucking bitch is dead, and she is not coming back unless I piss on her grave and unleash a voodoo spell on her monkey ass—you understand me? Now, I don't want to hear another word about how you miss her deadbeat ass! For the rest of the trip, I don't want you to do nothing but shut the fuck up and drive this piece of shit!"

Johnny knew Nicole was right. She might not have said it in the best of words, but it sounded like poetry. "You sure are right, sweetheart. I should learn how to keep my mouth shut and listen sometimes, but don't you worry. I just know things will look up for all of us as soon as we get to Vegas, and you will find yourself the biggest bag of coke you've ever seen in your fucking life."

After everything was patched up between them, they did nothing but listen to the radio and hope for the best luck that Vegas could bring them.

After about eight hours, Johnny's eyes began to get heavy, his back grew sore, and he knew it was a good idea to let Taryn take over behind the wheel. "Hey! Pothead! Put that joint out and take over driving. I'm so tired, and my back is sore, and all I want to do is get some sleep."

Taryn couldn't have been more excited to hear those words, and so she immediately jumped out of her seat and got behind the wheel.

"All right now, sweetheart, just keep going down this road, and it will take us straight into Viva Las Vegas!"

"You got it, Dad! Don't worry. I'm going to take us straight there, and we're all going to have a blast—OK! You just lie down in the back, and we will be there in no time."

Johnny quickly fell asleep, and after about a half hour, Nicole felt that it was time to get the party started a little bit more as they cruised down the highway, headed for Sin City. "Check it out, bitch! Want to do some bumps with me? I was waiting for that old fuck to pass out, or he would just be mooching off me again."

Taryn felt relieved to hear that her little sister, Nicole, had her favorite medicine in her purse, and she couldn't wait for her to bust it out. "Well, hell yeah! I'm not driving for my health here. If you want me to get us to Vegas in one piece, I'll need a little wake-up call."

"Funny you said that, Taryn, because this new shit is called the Rooster, and it will probably be the last Texas coke that you and I will do."

After hours had gone by, the bright lights of the Vegas strip were finally upon them. Their big wide eyes and huge smiles made it clear that they were happy to have made it to their destination.

"Wake up, you old piece of shit. We're finally here!" Nicole yelled, and she began shaking her dad's arm.

"Oh boy, Taryn, you did it! You got us here all safe and sound without fucking anything up, like you usually do!"

The three of them didn't have the slightest idea how they would make it in Vegas; there was never a particular plan for housing and expenses. Now, as they sat in their car across from the Golden Gate casino, with only a hundred bucks in each of their pockets, they all decided it would be best if they split up and met back at the car in three hours. There was so much entertainment everywhere, and they all knew they would not be interested in anything but their own choice. They all went their separate ways.

CHAPTER 3

Stanley, the Fuck-Up

Meanwhile, back in the town of Skank Hill, another troubled family had their struggles. They were the Barstool family, a family of five who had grown up and lived their entire lives around the town of Skank Hill. The Barstool family wasn't the average family that you would find around the corner. They had the reputation of being the absolute worst family in town. Skank Hill's population was only about fifty people, so any time they fucked up, every asshole in town would know about it, and they would never hear the end of their loud and endless lectures.

There was only one employed family member in the Barstool household, and it wasn't the father, Sanchez Barstool—he spent his days and nights out in his garage, drinking his life away. His only companion was his youngest son, Stanley, another drunken mess who had been following in his father's footsteps ever since he was born. Now, just like they always did, they were sitting in the garage, cracking open another bottle of rum.

"Son, I have some important news I need to tell you, so you'd better listen up! You know how we've been struggling, and it's been tough keeping up with bills. Now your lousy-ass stepmother and I have no other choice but to move out of this house and find something more affordable. But don't worry because it's still in town, so that means we don't have to say goodbye to Skank Hill."

Stanley didn't know if he should cry or hang himself at that moment. He had been dreaming of leaving Skank Hill for as long as he could remember, and just when he thought his father would move them all out of there, his hopes were once again crushed. "Goddamn it, Dad! What the fuck did you do this time? You drank all our rent money, didn't you? And you didn't even bother to give me one fucking drop, did you?"

Sanchez Barstool had been struggling with alcohol ever since his kids were born. His dream was to be a country rock star. Still, ever since his first wife told him she was pregnant, he knew his life was over. He had no other choice but to sell his guitar at a pawnshop so he could buy food for his new family and a bottle of rum to drown himself in for all the misery he was about to take in.

Sanchez was head of the household, but lots of times, he didn't seem to be playing with a full deck. That didn't matter because his loving family was always there to handle the family issues that he could not take on mentally by himself—such as his new wife, Amelia, a gold-digging bitch out of Wisconsin, who could not give a fuck whether he lived or died. Of course, she would never tell anybody that; instead, she put on a happy smile and pretended that she was the happiest wife on earth. Everybody in the house believed her lies, except for Stanley. Only he knew she was up to no good.

Still, he could do nothing about it because he was just as big a drunk as his father, and nobody took him seriously, not even his cross-dressing brother, Pauley, or his fat, lazy sister, Lacy. Then again, they never got along anyway.

Stanley Barstool felt like he wandered all alone, with no one to care for him. Every day, he would pray to God and ask why God had left him all alone in a town called Skank Hill, with a rotten family and a dead mother, who had been another drunk, just like him and his father—but she took the easy way out of life.

After dealing with Sanchez's crazed-out drunken ways for so many years, she couldn't take anymore. One night, she decided that it would be best if she just vanished from this world for good so she wouldn't have to deal with anybody's stupid shit. Late one night, without telling anybody, she took some chicken wire out of a box, where Sanchez kept all his sex toys, and then hanged herself in the front yard where everybody could see.

That was a sad time for Stanley. He wouldn't let it keep him down, but he always carried around the misery everywhere he went. Nobody wanted to hang out with him because he was too depressing. Now, he just continued with his life, hoping that one day, something or someone would save him from all the pain he went through day after day.

"So, what is this other place we're supposed to move to, Dad? And how long do we have until they kick us the fuck out? I bet you moved us to a real shithole, didn't you?"

Sanchez didn't want to hear any annoying questions at that moment. "Look here, you stupid fucking kid! You were not meant to have good things because you're nothing but a goddamn drunk like your mother! And you think you can just do anything you set your mind to? Forget it—you're nothing but a loser, just like your drunk-ass mama, and the only thing you're ever going to be good for is getting drunk and making a fool of yourself in front of anybody. You just shut the hell up, and let me guide this fucked-up family to where it needs to be!"

Stanley Barstool did nothing and said nothing. As usual, he continued to drink the night away with his drunken father in their lonesome garage. Still, as time went on, things only got worse and worse for Stanley Barstool, but he held on tight for as long as he could, wishing for the best for himself.

CHAPTER 4

Las Vegas

Three Hours Later

After trying to come out on top with only a hundred dollars in each of their pockets, the Cherry family had no other choice but to accept defeat and meet back at the car. They didn't feel too bad, though, knowing that all three of them had failed. What would lie ahead next for them was the question they would have to figure out for themselves.

"So, what the fuck do we do now, Dad?" Taryn shouted. "You worthless piece of shit—now we're stuck here in Vegas because you couldn't strike it rich for your family!"

Johnny felt he had no other choice but to quickly put her in her place. "You didn't do so well either, you crazed-out bitch! Don't point the finger at me! It's not my fault you lost your ass off. Maybe if you were a gorgeous little whore like your little sister, you would mean a little more to me as a daughter."

Taryn couldn't believe her ears. She had never heard her father talk about her that way. When she tried to take a swing at her dad's head, Nicole was there to stop her from doing so.

"Don't hit him, Taryn! Father's right; if you would just learn to loosen up a little bit and lie on your back from time to time, you could probably land yourself a good husband. Still, right now, since I'm the pro, I think you two should wait here at the car while I go back out and work my magic. We're going to need food, gas money, and a place to stay for the night so

14

we can figure shit out." Nicole wandered out into the night, leaving her family waiting patiently at the car while she went to the dirtiest corners to promote her sexy body to every horny scumbag in town.

"Good luck, my baby girl! Make your daddy super proud now!" Johnny called out as he waved her on with great spirit and cheer.

Taryn wasn't too happy with either of them, and so she just rolled her eyes and shook her head as she watched her little sister walk away. She just hoped Nicole knew what she was doing and would make it back safely.

As they waited for Nicole to come back, they sat on the street and debated how much they thought Nicole would make in an hour and what they would do with the money when she returned. Nicole would call it *putting in work for the family's emergency needs.*

"I think the bitch will make at least two hundred bucks in one hour, as long as she remembers not to bite the dick when she's giving a blow job. Word on the street is that she's not the best dick sucker in town," Taryn said as she rolled a joint for her father to smoke while they waited.

"Don't worry, Taryn. I know my daughter very well, and I know she will strike big tonight and make her daddy a great fortune. I taught her everything she needs to know about running the streets."

Taryn couldn't have been more upset at hearing all that. "Your daughter is a fucking whore, Dad! Don't give yourself the fucking Father of the Year award quite yet. To me, you have always been a worthless piece of shit ever since Mom's wood-chipper accident—or should I say, *your* and Mom's wood chipper accident."

Johnny knew what she was talking about, but he tried not to get too deep into the past. He exclaimed, "Look here, Taryn! It was an accident, really. I didn't mean to push her in, she just drove me so fucking mad, and I couldn't help myself. It just happened."

Taryn wouldn't let him off that easily. "You didn't just push her, Dad. You picked her up and threw her into the fucking thing. Then when you were done, you just stood tall with your chest out and with a smile on your face as you slowly watched her die! I will never get her fucking screams out of my head, you crazy fuck!"

Johnny didn't have much to say after Taryn laid it all down on him as she did. Still, he tried. "Well, what the fuck were you doing? You always knew I was crazy, so why didn't you just come to her rescue instead of standing around with your thumb up your ass?"

"I was just a little girl, you stupid fuck! How did you expect me to jump in and save her?"

After almost hearing her cry, Johnny didn't want to hear her bitching and moaning anymore, so he changed the subject of their conversation as quickly as possible. "OK! I get it! I'm the worst fucking father you could ever have. You probably wished you had a much better family from the day you were born, but you'll have to face it, cupcake! You are in this family—a family that has a murdering father and a whore for a sister! So just bite your tongue and get used to it because that's reality and also your family. In other words, let's just smoke on that joint you're rolling and call a truce for the rest of the night."

No more words needed to be said. They lit up the joint and smoked away as they waited for Nicole to return from her hard night of ass banging and hand jobs.

It didn't take Nicole too long to connect with her first customer. She was such a professional that she could easily identify an idiot, someone she knew she could hustle and take for everything he was worth. That poor son of a bitch was nothing but a scrubby mop boy, working as a janitor at a public bathroom somewhere on the side of the road. His name was Vincent, but he never liked that name. He tried his very best to get his mother and boss to call him Crazy V, but they both just told him to shut the fuck up and go piss up a tree.

Vincent never had any friends. All he ever did was sleep on his mother's couch and work as a mop boy, hoping every second that he could one day get fucked in the ass by a beautiful woman. Vincent wasn't a young man, but he wasn't too old either; he was somewhat in his midthirties but still had never been laid. When he met Nicole, he saw nothing but chemistry sparkling in the air. He was sure that she felt the same way about him, but just like any other ordinary guy who was gullible, he would find out the truth the hard way.

"Hey, there, handsome. What you doin' out here all by your lonesome on such a beautiful night?"

Vincent couldn't believe she was talking to him. He just about came in his pants at the sound of her beautiful voice, but Vincent knew he had to pull it together, or he just might remain a virgin for the rest of his life. "I work here, miss. Now let me tell you something—there isn't any other place I would rather work than here at this shithole bathroom facility! It is the best damn job I ever scored in my whole life."

Nicole couldn't believe how easy this was going to be. He was a much bigger loser than she expected, and she knew she could work him for a good price without spreading her legs. "You feel like taking a break from work and buying a lady a nice breakfast somewhere?"

Vincent knew he could get in serious trouble if he left his workstation unattended, but he couldn't care less because this could be his chance to get laid for the first time in his life. There was no way in hell he would let this opportunity slip out of his hands. "Hell yeah, I do! Let me pull my car out front, and off to Burger Chef we go!"

Nicole immediately began to wonder how long it would take her to make this guy give her everything he had. She didn't want her father and sister to wait too long for her in the middle of the night.

Before she knew it, Vincent pulled up in a Volkswagen Bus. "Come on, bitch, get in! Burger Chef is not going to wait all fucking day for us!"

Nicole climbed into the Volkswagen, and they went off. Nicole was thrilled by how Vincent had decorated the inside of his vehicle. "Wow, Vincent! I like the Christmas lights you hung up and all the porn pictures you cut out of magazines and pasted on the walls. You sure know how to make a woman feel right at home."

A smile rose on Vincent's face as they continued down the road. "Thank you. I appreciate that because everybody I know hates this Volkswagen, except my mother. I catch her almost all the time out in this Volk's bus, fingering herself to these pictures."

"Your mama sure sounds like a wonderful lady. I bet she cares a lot about you." Nicole said as she moved toward Vincent, sitting much closer to him so she could put her hand down his pants for a little hand job.

"Goddamn, woman! You know how to please a man so very well!"

Nicole smiled and continued. "Thank you, Vincent. My daddy taught me everything I needed to know to run the streets."

"Well, in that case, thank God for your daddy doing so well in raising his daughter to be the best damn daughter any father could ever have."

Once again, Nicole smiled at Vincent and continued. "Thank you, Vincent. My father would love to hear those words—if he wasn't in a coma."

As soon as Vincent heard those words, he quickly made her stop everything. "I'm so sorry to hear that, baby. Is there anything I can do?"

Nicole's lie was working out perfectly, so she continued to bullshit him as much as possible. "The doctor is trying everything he can do, but our medical insurance does not cover drunk driving accidents. That's why I'm out here on the streets, trying to raise money to keep him alive. If they don't have a certain amount of money by tomorrow morning, they said they would have no other choice but to pull the plug on him."

Vincent felt sorry for Nicole's father and wished he could help. Still, the only thing that came to mind was a generous handout, without making her give anything in return. Even that required serious thought because it was more about his needs than hers, and he didn't want to remain a virgin for the rest of his life. "Look here, Nicole, maybe we don't have to go to Burger Chef. I was thinking, off the top of my head, that maybe we could skip the cheeseburgers and go straight to fucking your brains out in this bad-ass Volk's bus! And when it's all said and done, I will put money down on your father's sorry, soon-to-be-dead ass and send you on your way before they pull the plug on him. Now is that a deal or what? I get what I need, and you get what you want."

Nicole had planned from the beginning that she would take advantage of him without giving up any sex whatsoever, but now it seemed that Vincent was taking advantage of her. *How the hell could I have let this happen?* she wondered, but she didn't let the situation affect her. She had no other choice but to help provide money for her family, who was waiting for her back in the car. "That sounds like a great deal, baby. Maybe you should pull over somewhere dark and quiet so nobody can see or hear us fucking!"

Vincent couldn't wait another second to finally stick his dick in a woman for the very first time in his life. "Don't you worry now, darling. I'm going to find us the best goddamn place to have sweet doggy-style sex, and that place is on my mama's couch!"

Nicole was pissed off deep inside, but she could not let Vincent know because she needed the money. She didn't want to hurt his feelings, but she tried to persuade him anyway. "You sure you want to lose your virginity on your mama's couch? What if she walks in on us? Don't you think we should find a place where we could be alone?" She began rubbing her hands back and forth on his leg.

"Don't worry; she won't walk in, and even if she does, the only thing she will do is watch a little, and then she will go away."

Nicole had no other choice. She had to stop him in his tracks right then and there before they reached his street. "OK, Vincent, I'm not going to fuck you on your mama's couch while your mother watches us. It's bad enough that I let my father watch my ex-boyfriends and me doing it from time to time. In other words, Vincent, you're going to have to think of another place, or you can forget about us fucking tonight."

Vincent wasn't sure where he could take her. His mama's house and the bathroom facility were the only two places he knew. Out of frustration, he decided it would be best to stop the Volks on the side of the road and talk things out with Nicole. "OK, I give up! I don't know where else I can bring you to make you feel right at home, so I guess I will remain a virgin!"

Nicole felt sorry for him because of his stupidity. She knew she could retake the advantage over him at that very moment. "When I said to find us a place to go fuck, I didn't mean a Holiday Inn or your mama's couch. I just meant finding a place to park this piece of shit! We have a full-size Volk's bus, Vincent! We can just fuck in the back."

The look on Vincent's face couldn't have grown happier after hearing Nicole's bright, slutty scheme. "Oh boy, that's such a wonderful idea! Why the hell couldn't I have thought of that in the first place?"

Nicole only shrugged her shoulders as she slowly climbed her way into the back of the Volks bus. "Are you coming, Vincent? Or are you going to sit behind the wheel all day, wondering what pussy could feel like?"

She didn't have to say anymore because Vincent was up in a heartbeat and into the back seat. "Bitch, you don't have to tell me twice. I'm right here and ready to go! So please tell me how this works and which hole I put it in."

Vincent was serious, but Nicole laughed in his face, not believing that she was talking to a full-grown man who hadn't been laid in his life. "Use your fucking head, Vincent. Which hole do you think your dick goes into? And don't even think about coming in from the back because a first-timer like you couldn't handle that! Let me run you through the basics so you don't fuck up anything! First things first, you need to start taking off your clothes because I have already taken off mine. Second, strap a condom to your cock—you're going to need one of those, Vincent."

"Oh shit! I don't have a condom, and I wouldn't know how to use one of those things even if I had one."

Vincent was useless to Nicole; she couldn't wait to get him over with. He was the dumbest customer she had ever gotten herself involved with, and she knew she would never get mixed up with someone this stupid ever again. "OK, Vincent! We will skip to step three because not too many people use condoms these days anyway. Still, they probably should because it causes bad future STD events for all the new people out there, trying to get their fuck on, but then again, it's the seventies, so what's the worst that can happen?"

With them both naked in the back of Vincent's Volk's bus, Nicole lay there with her legs spread open, getting ready to guide Vincent's dick into the kingdom of heaven. "This is it, Vincent! This is your moment! All you must do now is just put your cock into this wet slippery hole right here, and you will finally be a whole new man. You will never have to worry about being a worthless fucking loser ever again!"

Vincent's heart was racing so fast that he could hardly breathe, and he had to stop for a short minute to take a few breaths.

Nicole couldn't believe that Vincent was choking from the pressure right in the middle of what was his best moment in his whole life. She needed to snap him back to reality by slapping him in the face.

"Ow! That hurt! What the hell has gotten into you?" Vincent yelled.

Nicole was so frustrated with him that she felt she had no choice but to do it again. "You need to wake the fuck up, Vincent, and realize that there is some fucking pussy in your face. You need to be a man and learn how to fuck it! Now come on, Vincent, get your shit together, or you're going to regret this very moment for the rest of your pathetic life. You will never have the confidence to talk to another woman again! You won't even look at another woman because your mind will no longer find them attractive. Then, you will probably wind up turning gay and marrying a big dude named Bubba Joe, and he will have no problem finding your hole and plugging you up until you scream like a little ragged bitch, just like your whore mother! And he will always tell you what to do because you'll be the female in the relationship. You will end up doing nothing but cleaning after him and sucking his fucking dick every time he asks for it! Now is that the kind of lifestyle you want to live with forever and ever?"

Right then and there, Vincent finally snapped out of it. "Hell, no, I don't want that kind of lifestyle! I want to marry you so I can be your bitch instead, and you will never have to worry about me running off and cheating on you because there is no other woman who would want anything to do with me in the first place."

Nicole couldn't take it anymore. Vincent was pissing her off, and raping him was the only thing on her mind. "Oh, get over yourself, Vincent! I said I would fuck you, not marry you. You're lucky even to get that, so just lie on your back, hold still, and don't say a fucking word. I will be done raping your little monkey ass in no time."

A smile quickly came to Vincent's face. "Oh boy! I don't believe this is finally happening. I wish I had my camera to take pictures of your fine ass. That way, I can have something to always jack off to later."

Nicole didn't like any of Vincent's stupid, annoying humor. She felt that he needed a whacking right across the face, so without warning, she threw a quick jab with her left arm across his nose, making him bleed instantly and even drawing a tear down his cheek.

"Why the fuck did you do that?" Vincent yelled, trying his best to remember what he had done wrong.

"Look, Vincent, you need to take this sex shit more seriously! Making love is supposed to be a very romantic thing."

Once again, Vincent responded stupidly. "That's not what I was taught! I was told that the female twat hole was only there for every man's pleasure, just a place to plant your seeds and skip out of town just before the baby arrives."

There was no telling how much anger was running inside Nicole's mind at that very moment. She started to feel that there was no need to fulfill Vincent's lonely virgin dreams, so she needed to think of a way to collect the money and ditch him at the same time. "Now, you'd better shut up and strip off all those clothes, Vincent. We finally need to make you a man."

And so, he did, and it took him no longer than ten seconds.

"Now that you're done with that, I need you to go outside and make sure all the tires have enough air in each of them, and I need that done right now."

Vincent wasn't sure what the tires had to do with his finally getting laid. "But I'm already naked and ready for you, baby! I'm not going outside to do all that stupid shit right now. What's the use of doing all that?"

Nicole didn't have to do too much but play dumb. "It just makes me feel safer, Vincent, knowing that all the tires have air in them while we are fucking. Sometimes, tires can pop if you're fucking too hard, and I don't wish to be stranded with you!"

Vincent had no choice but to do what Nicole had asked because not keeping her happy could ruin his chances with her tonight. He did not want to end the time of his life in disappointment. "OK, bitch! I'll do this one little thing, and you'd better be satisfied and ready to boogie when I get back, and I fucking mean it!" And so, Vincent did what she asked, and as he stormed out of the Volks to check every tire, all angry and naked, he heard the sound of the Volks bus engine starting up, and it began driving away. "Hey, bitch! What the fuck you think you're doing? Get your stupid, ragged whore ass back here now! That's my fucking Volk's bus, you dumb fucked-up bitch!"

But there was no turning back for Nicole. Her family was waiting for her in the middle of the parking lot, and she needed to get back to them as soon as possible. Everything couldn't have gone better; she didn't have to give up the goods, and she ended up with more money and value than she expected. "I got this fool's Volk's bus. I got this fool's money, and I didn't even have to give him any play. Oh my Lord, what a fucking night," Nicole yelled as she looked in the rearview mirror to see Vincent's naked ass standing on the side of the road, shaking his fist in anger. "See you later, you sorry-ass motherfucker! I hope your mama whips your motherfucking ass, you little faggot-ass bitch."

Off she went in a stolen Volk's bus, and when she arrived at the parking lot where her father and sister were waiting, she felt good to be near her family and could not wait to show them everything she had scored. "Hey, guys, I'm back!" she shouted out the window as she pulled up in the Volks right next to them.

"Where in the hell did you get this thing?" her father asked; he looked desperate to test drive it.

"Let's just say I cut a good deal with this dude off the street. It was a real steal."

After hearing that, her father didn't care about how she got the Volks, just if she was OK and would permit him to test drive it. "Say there, my little angel daughter, do you think it would be OK for me to take this out for a spin?"

But Taryn thought it would be best if they all figured out what to do about their living status. "Come on, you guys, quit fooling around! We still need to figure out where the fuck we are going to live! We are in the middle of Las Vegas and were fucking homeless! And so, I think it's best if we figure out what the fuck we're going to do first, before we do any test driving." Taryn had a good point, and they all knew it

Out of nowhere, when they needed the help the most, a strange old man came from behind them and startled all three of them. "Excuse me, folks! I couldn't help overhearing that you are having trouble finding a place to stay. I bet you guys lost your asses out here, and now you don't have any place to go or anything to show for it. Is that correct?"

The only thing the three of them could do was just stand there and look at each other in silence.

"I might know a place where you all can stay. It's a place where all losers like you go when they bust out because Sin City was too much for them—but that's only if you're interested."

Taryn didn't want her father or sister to say a word because she knew they would say something stupid to scare the man away or to get them into a deeper hole than the one they were already in. She felt she had no choice but to speak for all three of them. "That sounds like a wonderful offer, sir, but if you don't mind me asking, what's your name and what is this place that you're talking about?"

The old man stuck his chest out and grinned. "My name is Peter—Peter Wrinkled Sack—and I'll tell you exactly the place I'm talking about. It's not a place, really; it's a town—and a very fine one too, one you all could afford, especially in a time like this. It's a town called Skank Hill, a small town just about 150 miles from here, headed north toward Carson City."

"How do you know about this place?" Taryn asked.

"Well, believe it or not, miss, it's my hometown, where I was born and raised, and I wouldn't want to live anywhere else! And you all look like good-hearted people. I wouldn't mind showing you the way and showing you around when we get there. I already have a friend who has a place up for grabs—well, it will be as soon as he kicks a poor drunken family out to the curb. Those stupid fucks haven't paid rent in years! But once again, that's only if you all are interested."

Taryn didn't know exactly what to say; she knew she needed a second opinion from her family. "If you don't mind, sir, I will need a moment to talk things over with my two little assistants."

"Go on ahead, miss. Take as long as you want. I'll be standing over here, smoking this big crack ball! Best shit in Sin City!" the old man said.

Taryn paid him no attention and began talking things over with her family. "OK, guys, what do you think? I mean, we have no other option. Maybe we give the old man a chance and see how we can benefit from it. It just might be a gold mine."

Even though Johnny's suggestion didn't mean shit to either Taryn or Nicole, he still wanted to speak his mind. "I don't know about this guy. I think it's best that we just check into a shelter and search for jobs instead."

Right away, Taryn needed to lay it down to her father on how it would all go down. "Look here, old man! Don't be going fucking soft on me because we are going through with this shit, and I don't want to hear you complain. Your idea was good, but it failed, so now poor Nicole and me need to clean up the mess you started! Shut the fuck up and get into our brand-new Volk bus because we are going to Skank Hill!"

That was all that was said between a father and his daughter at that very moment. Johnny said absolutely nothing as he stood there and watched them deal with Old Man Peter Wrinkled Sack.

"OK, Mr. Wrinkled Sack, you can count us in. Please show us how."

Peter couldn't have been happier. His face lit up with a smile, and he smoked the last bit of his crack on the bottom of his filthy glass pipe. "Well then, all right, all right strangers. Let's saddle up our horses and get on the road! I drive pretty fast, so hopefully you can catch up."

Taryn didn't think about how fast Peter Wrinkled Sack could drive. Still, when she saw him strolling over to his Chevrolet Chevelle, she knew that neither the Ford Pinto nor their new Volk bus had a good chance against Peter Wrinkled Sack in his awesome hot rod. "All right, everyone, I'll drive our piece of shit, and Nicole, you and Dad can ride together in your new Volk. Please make sure Dad drives because he has been wanting to test drive it, and most of all, I don't want to hear him bitch!"

Nicole had no problem doing what Taryn had directed because she didn't want to hear their dad bitching either. After everyone was packed and ready to go, they started their cars and were on their way.

CHAPTER 5

Moving Day for the Barstool Family

It was a sad day at the Barstool household. They had no other choice but to pack up their belongings and leave.

Stanley's father, Sanchez, however, was at a critical appointment at the real estate office and was in the middle of closing a deal with a crooked real estate agent named Dustin, a mentally retarded junkie from the sticks of Kentucky.

"All right, Mr. Barstool. I must inform you that there are no homes outside the state of Nevada or any other city or town in Nevada that would be willing to take on you and your poor, fucked-up family because their dad is too much of a drunken wreck to have good things in hand, like a down payment and deposit, or even good credit, or something showing that you're a good citizen who hasn't been in trouble with the law more than twenty-five times in a year. Those would be really nice documents to have right now, Mr. Barstool, but unfortunately for you, you don't have any of those. The only thing I could dig up that would be perfect for you and your family at a time like this is the old western whorehouse, just only a few blocks from where you're staying. I think you and your loving family would like it there very much, and it's even cheaper than where you're staying now. That means, sir, that you can buy three times more booze than you're buying now! I'm also required by the law to inform you about the history of the house and all the fixing it needs."

Sanchez was so excited to hear how much money he could save for his booze that he didn't want to hear any more. "All right, Dusty—Dustin—if this is the only house for my family and me and can save me money to buy all the liquor I need, I'll take it!"

"But sir, please! I must tell you about the strange paranormal activity that the residents of this place have seen and heard. They say this place is fucked up in a very intense, evil way."

Still, Sanchez couldn't be bothered to listen to what Dustin had to say. "I have no time to hear no fucking ghost story. Everyone who checked out of that place was probably drinking more than I do, and that's why they couldn't stay there no longer because they would rather buy booze than pay their fucking rent!"

Now that Sanchez had made up his mind about getting the house, Dustin felt his job was done. There was no need to discuss the strange house with Sanchez, and so with nothing more to do than shake hands and sign papers, Sanchez accepted the only offer they had and closed the deal.

"Thank you so much, sir. You have no idea how much this house means to my family and me. I pray to the Lord that they make more men like you."

Dustin kicked his feet up on his office desk and slammed a huge amount of heroin into his arm, leaving the syringe to dangle and bleed. "Enjoy the house, Mr. Barstool, and don't forget to send me your pregnant daughter's phone number because I would love to tap that ass!"

"Don't worry, sir! I'll have that number for you tomorrow morning, and I'll even tell her to throw in a hand job."

Now that it was a done deal and everything was squared away, Sanchez was ready to tell his family what he felt was great news. "Guess what, my loving family? I have awesome-possum news! A house just opened up for us right here in Skank Hill. They said it might need a little fixing up, but we can handle that, right? And another great thing is that it's only a few blocks down the street from our home here. The real estate guy said it used to be an old western whorehouse, and there could be some scary, horny ghosts wanting to rape your asses in your sleep! But I just told him to shut the fuck up and toss me the keys to the house—that little sack of shit! After I said that, he shook in his boots like a little bitch and handed me the key."

The family knew he was lying, and poor Stanley had to say something because the rest of the family didn't speak. "Yeah, right, Dad" Stanley shouted at the top of his lungs. "First of all, you would never have the guts to talk to someone like that, and second of all, why the fuck did you agree to move us in that house? Do you have any idea what kind of crazy shit goes on there? You should have listened to that fucking real estate dude. That place is evil and probably on its last legs and covered in termites!"

His father only shrugged his shoulders and played it off as if he'd done nothing wrong. "Oh, quit your bitching, son. There is nothing wrong with the house. It's just a stupid ghost story planted in everybody's head, and it's not true! And there is nothing physically wrong with. It's either because it's as stiff as a rock or clean as a whistle."

That wasn't convincing enough for Stanley. "Did he even take you out to the place and show you around, or did you just buy all his bullshit?"

Sanchez couldn't believe he was having such a conversation with his son Stanley and knew he had to end it and get the rest of the family involved. "Oh, shut the fuck up, Stanley! Quit being a party pooper and trying to spoil it for the rest of us! Your lazy-ass sister, Lacy, and your queer-bait brother, Pauley, like the idea of us moving in there, and so does your new stepmama, Amelia! So you'd better get your shit together and start liking it too, boy, because we are moving there today. Pack up your shit because the collection agency is only giving us so much time to move out, and we can only bring so much stuff."

"What's the fucking hurry? Aren't they supposed to give us, like, a forty-five-day notice or something?" Stanley asked.

"Yes, son, they did, but I didn't say anything to you. I was sure I could figure everything out before the shit hit the fan, but I failed, as a father, to do that, and I'm very sorry to you all. I should have told you guys sooner, but I was just too ashamed to face any of you."

Poor, lazy Lacy tried her best to comfort her father right away. "Don't worry, Dad. We still love you."

Stanley never liked it when his sister came to his father with open arms, feeling sorry for him. "Quit trying to make the old man feel warm inside because that piece of shit is moving his whole family into a whorehouse!"

Lacy ignored her brother and continued her good-hearted ways. "Don't you mind what your little jackass son says because together we will make that whorehouse into the best family home ever. It will be the best goddamn family whorehouse anyone has ever seen!" Lacy said. She looked over at Stanley with a mean, dirty look, as if he was the worst son on the face of the planet.

"Don't give me that look, you crazy bitch! Or I'll slap the living dog shit out of your ass!"

"Shut up, Stanley, before I call up T-Bone and have him stick your head in the cat litter box again!"

T-Bone was Lacy's baby's daddy, and he never got along with Stanley because T-Bone thought Stanley was a strange piece of shit. Stanley always had to take a beating from T-Bone. After T-Bone and Lacy broke up, Stanley couldn't have been happier.

"You can call up that motherfucker all you want, but it ain't be like the last time! This time, I'm going to knock him on his ass and make him eat cat shit out of a fucking box and see how he likes it!"

Their father couldn't stand to hear anymore. "OK, you two, I do not have to listen to this shit! Both of you settle down, or I'm going to have to pull out the strap, just like the good old days. I know you both know what I mean when I'm talking about the good old days! Let's just cut the shit and start packing because we need to be out as soon as possible. Pack up whatever you need and your valuables, and leave the rest for the next family moving in here."

"Oh, Dad, this is such a sad day for us," Lacy cried. "Even though we are moving into a wonderful whorehouse, I still wish we didn't have to leave here so soon. This place is filled with so many memories."

Sanchez had to keep her moving and packing with his unusual motivational ways. "Quit your goddamn crying, or I'm going to give you something to cry about, bitch. And I fucking mean it. I'll smack you real hard with my fist and leave a permanent shit mark right in the middle of your fucking forehead!"

During Sanchez's motivational speech, Stanley couldn't help laughing. "That's right, bitch! Pack your shit and get the fuck out of the house!" he shouted, trying to catch his breath from laughing so hard.

"Shut the fuck up, Stanley. You're moving out too, dumbass! You'd better pack your shit and get out as well!"

Once again, Sanchez was getting annoyed by their bickering back and forth and knew he had to lay down the law. "You two both better shut the fuck up and pack your shit! Everybody in this motherfucking house is going out and moving into a beautiful whorehouse! Let's just come together and try to get shit done! Goddamn it, man!"

There was no more fighting after hearing all that; they just did what their father told them to do, and before they knew it, they were ready to journey off to live in their new home.

"Let's go, you guys. Another beautiful home awaits us," Sanchez said with joy.

The rest of them stared out the back window, saying their last goodbyes to their old home as Sanchez slowly drove away.

It didn't take long for the Barstool family to arrive at their new home— it was just a few blocks down the street, and after only a couple of minutes of driving, they were there. Sanchez was sure that the real estate agent would have handled some of the landscape issues because the house itself still didn't look like it was ready for any family to move in. The grass in the yard was long and shaggy, and every window and door was still boarded up.

"Those motherfuckers! They said they would have the house ready and cozy for us, but it looks like we will have to welcome ourselves to this place. It's a house anyway, right?"

The others paid no attention to their father as they searched for tools in the trunk of their car to pry the two-by-fours off the windows.

"Goddamn it, Dad! You think I enjoy doing hard labor? I'm tired of cleaning after your mess because you fucked up. We should make you pry off all these fucking two-by-fours!" Stanley complained.

Sanchez couldn't let his son get away with that sassiness. "Oh, quit your fucking bellyaching, boy! I have cleaned after your mess plenty of times, so stop pretending that your shit ain't dirty! Remember that time when you got so drunk and passed out on your auntie's couch and pissed all over it? That fucking bitch made me buy her another one, which cost eight hundred dollars! It should have been you buying her a new fucking couch, but it wasn't because I did, so fuck you! I can name a few other drunken incidents on your ass, if you like. But I think it would be best for us to work together, like we were supposed to do from the beginning. Let's just do that."

There was no more said after that. They all came together and worked as a team.

CHAPTER 6

Moving Day for the Cherry Family

It was all fun and games as the Cherry family cruised down the highway as fast as they could, like it was an Indy 500 speed race, but no one could catch up to Peter Wrinkled Sack and his hot rod. He was way ahead of them all.

Johnny didn't care because he was having the time of his life, testing out the new Volk bus that Nicole had stolen. "Come on, bitch! Come on—show me what you got!" Johnny shouted, with his head sticking out the window, trying his best to ram them from the side.

"Quit fucking around, Dad! You're not funny! I swear if you put one dent into that Volk bus, I'm going to rip your fucking nuts off!" Taryn yelled. But she didn't let her father's foolish games bother her too much; she was so happy that they were on their way to a new home for all of them.

They were all driving at around seventy-five miles an hour, and before they knew it, they were halfway there—and then a little bad luck fell into their laps. The Volks bus got a flat tire, and it couldn't have come at a worse time. Everybody heard the pop, especially Nicole and her father, Johnny. It came from the Volks bus's left back tire, and they had no other choice but to pull over to the side and wave everybody down to come back and help.

"What the fuck did you hit, Dad? Goddamn it, I knew I shouldn't have let you drive!" Nicole yelled.

"I didn't hit anything, you dumb bitch, so don't dare yell at me! I bet all these tires are worn out, and you didn't even know."

Nicole's wouldn't allow her father to point the finger at her. "Don't you blame me. If you knew how to drive, this would never have happened."

Johnny started to feel bad about the situation and wondered if it was his fault. "Fuck, man, I can never do anything right for my kids!" he muttered as he sat on the curb, waiting for the others to come back to give them a hand.

"Don't get too comfortable on that curb, Dad! You're going to fix this flat tire because I sure don't know how, and I wouldn't do it, even if I knew."

All poor Johnny could do was sit there silently and agree to everything she said. "Yes, Nicole, no problem, I think there is a jack and a lug wrench somewhere in the Volks—at least, there should be. I believe every vehicle should come with one, and if it doesn't, then don't worry because I know I have one in the Pinto."

"What are you and Dad doing, Nicole? Why did you stop?" Taryn asked as she slowly pulled up next to them.

"Dad hit something on the road, and now we have a flat tire!" Nichole said angrily.

Peter apparently had much more important things to do and could not wait for them one second—at least, that's what he told them. The truth was that he had nothing else better to do with the rest of his day but to go home and whack off to Linda Ronstadt pictures. He was such a big fan of her music, and from time to time, he would play with his balls while singing "Different Drum."

"Look, you guys, I have no time to sit around and watch you fix a tire. I told you guys I would bring you to this town and hook you up with a spot, and that's what I plan to do. Why don't you guys just leave the Volks here, and maybe you can come back and get it later. I have much shit I must do today. I am a very busy man."

After hearing all that, Nicole had no choice but to leave behind the Volks bus that she claimed she had worked so hard for. "Goddamn it! What a waste of time, going out and hustling this thing. I have no choice now but to leave it here on the side of the highway and hope no one takes it."

Taryn didn't think about her precious Volks; all she could do was roll her eyes. "Oh, quit your bitching! You didn't even buy the fucking thing. Besides, it looks like a ridiculous piece of shit anyway. I wouldn't be caught dead driving it! Maybe you should look at it this way—if the Volks is still standing tall on the side of the highway when you get back, then it was meant to be, and if it's not, then it was never meant to be yours—from the start."

Leaving the Volks bus behind was a little hard for Nicole because she never had owned a vehicle of her own—if she said she did, she had lied about it.

"Don't worry, Nicole," Taryn said. "Me and you will get another one once we get to Skank Hill, and I'll even let you pick it out. Deal?"

Nicole knew the Volks bus wasn't the best vehicle to drive, and it wasn't worth arguing over either, so she slowly looked up to her sister, Taryn, with a smile, and they shook on it. "OK, Taryn, but you'd better let me pick it out, just like you said. I'm not going to go cheap about it either. I'm going to pick the best and most expensive vehicle in Skank Hill, whether you like it or not."

Taryn knew that she had to say yes and nod her head to everything Nicole was demanding so that she would shut up and get in the car. They had already wasted time looking stupid, and Peter Wrinkled Sack would not wait any longer.

"Hey now! Let's get back on the road. I got to get home and jerk my dick off—I mean, I have much shit to do, so let's go!" Peter said as he sat in his car, honking his horn, looking rude and impatient.

"Yeah, OK, we're coming!" Taryn yelled. "Come on, Nicole, we got to get going. I don't want this old man to start tripping, or he just might give up the house to somebody else or perhaps another family, and we can't allow that to happen. Let's move the fuck on."

Now, with all the small drama behind them, they quickly piled into the Pinto and finally got on the road.

"It's about goddamn time," said Old Man Peter to himself.

They only had about an hour and a half of driving to go, and with Peter driving so fast in his hot rod Chevelle, it was hard to keep up in their slow-riding Pinto.

"My God, he is driving too fast! He better not try to ditch us deliberately to be an asshole!" Nicole grumbled.

Tarryn wasn't worried, and she made sure that her kid sister would not worry so much either. "Don't worry about Old Man Peter! Usually, men who drive fast cars are nothing but show-offs because they have small dicks. If he even thinks about trying to ditch us, I'll run over his precious little car with a fucking bulldozer!"

"Amen to that!" Johnny said.

"Dad, stay the fuck out of this! This is a bitches-only conversation, so please don't be rude."

And so, with no questions asked, he did exactly what she said. "I'm sorry, Taryn. I won't say another word unless you ask me."

"That's right, bitch. Stay quiet because we don't need any man getting into our business. Isn't that right, Nicole?"

The way Taryn provoked her father from time to time made Nicole laugh. "Oh, Taryn, leave him alone. He's only trying his best, but we both know that he will never get that Father of the Year trophy because he will most likely get the Drunk of the Year trophy, huh, Dad?"

"You two better keep your fucking mouths shut! Neither of you knows what it's like to be a single father with two delinquent shit daughters who do nothing but cause trouble. Sometimes I wonder if you two bitches are my real kids or if your mama had an affair with a deranged mule!"

Conversations like that always brought the family closer, and Taryn could never get enough of it. "Excuse me, asshole, but I think that Mom would have been better off with a mule because they have more common sense than you and probably have bigger dicks! Mom would always bitch to us about how small your dick was, every night before she tucked us in bed. It was disturbing, knowing that was the only thing she had to talk about, but we all know she used to get like that every time she came down from her high. Maybe if she had a better husband looking out for her, Dad, she wouldn't have had to turn to crack for all her problems, but you didn't give a shit, and that's why her so-called wood-chipper accident happened. All you can do now is keep quiet about it, as if you had nothing to do with it, while me and poor Nicole must suffer for it! Do you have any idea what it's like to grow up with a dead mother and a fucked-up father like you? It can drive any bitch crazy! You stupid piece of shit! But you don't care, and you probably won't even say anything because you want to be the better man and try your best to stay humble and shit, right?"

Sitting by himself in the back seat of the Pinto, listing to Taryn and Nicole talk shit about him, made Johnny feel very uncomfortable, and he hoped that he wouldn't say the wrong thing to make the situation worse. "Why must there always be a fucking fight between us? I'm sorry I'm not the greatest father that you two deserve. I'm not even the best person for myself, but I'm trying hard to get to that point, if you two would let me! I'm not going to be in your lives forever because I could be closer to death sooner than you guys think. Then you two will be alone. That means you will have two dead parents instead of one, so think about that shit too! You have a dead whore mother, but you will also have a dead junkie father! And then you two can tell your future hoodlum kids on Christmas Day that they won't be getting any presents from their grandparents because they are a couple of fucking lowlifes who pissed away their dreams on crack, heroin, and bitching and fighting every second of their days!"

Johnny felt excellent to release all his emotions; he had seen multiple psychiatrists who had always encouraged him to do that as much as possible to keep stable. Unfortunately for poor old Johnny, his daughter was a real nasty bitch who didn't give a fuck about his feelings.

"So, what's up, dude? Because you're an old man, I'm supposed to take a minute out of my time to give a fuck about your feelings? Fuck you and your goddamn doctors, Dad! I'm a self-made bitch, old-timer! Go lean on someone else's shoulder with all that trying-to-be-the-good-dad shit!"

It was best for poor Johnny not to say any more because he knew there was no winning an argument against someone as fucked up as his daughter. It felt like his dead wife's soul lived through his daughter's body to get back at him for her slow, tortured murder that he unleashed on her many years ago.

"Skank Hill, here we come, everybody!" Nicole yelled as she pulled out a few more bumps of coke from her purse for the second time of the trip.

"Where the fuck did you score this shit, Nicole? I thought we did the last of our old Texas shit!"

"You should know me by now, girl. I'm always one step ahead of you when it comes to scoring dope, and I always will be, so please don't try to keep up because you will just get burned, baby, burned. Ha-ha-ha!"

As soon as Taryn saw those thick powdered lines laying peacefully on Nicole's brand-new *Playboy* magazine, she didn't give a fuck where her kid sister got the shit. Every time she looked in the mirror, she saw her father's sad face staring back at her. He probably hoped that sweet little daughter would be kind enough to share a few bumps with her old man. Still, she decided not to. "Normally, I would always share with you, Dad, but because you have been acting like a little bitch lately, I think it's best that you just sit on the sidelines on this one because that's where I feel you're needed. Besides, there is nothing I would rather see than a drug addict without his medicine in the morning."

Johnny couldn't believe that his daughter would turn against him like that in the worst times. He had no idea where the crazy old man was taking him—if he was taking them to where he said he was—and at the same time, he had to sit in the back seat of the car throughout the rest of the trip without any sort of narcotics. "You filthy bitch! I'm your father, goddamn it, and you should never turn your back on family! Pass that fucking coke back this way, please. I have mental issues too—don't leave me out! Remember all the times I shared with you guys! You're very welcome, and I hope you two don't mind sharing some of that with your old man!"

Nicole had no choice but to say to her sister, "Now what do we do, Taryn? The fucking old man is desperate and needs a quick fix! You think we should help him or just say fuck him and let him ride it out until we get to town?"

"You two better fucking not," Johnny whispered to himself.

"Dad's right, Nicole. He has been there for us many times when we were in need, so we should help him now."

"But he was the asshole who got us hooked on all kinds of drugs. It's his fault that we were mentally in need of drugs every fucking day!" Nicole replied quickly.

Taryn could not let Nicole hold any kind of grudge against their father for the mistakes he regretfully had made years ago. "Yes, Nicole, I know he was the asshole who got both of us hooked on all this shit in the first place! But what he did to Mom right in front of our eyes was the craziest shit that I have ever seen in my life, and there was no fucking way I could face reality without drugs from that moment on! And neither could you, so let's not play the blame game right now. Sooner or later, down the road, we are going to be dry and in need. I don't want to worry about this piece of shit in the back seat being all stingy with the dope when he has it and we don't."

Nicole knew Taryn was right. For the rest of the trip, she tried her very best to make peace with her father so there would be no more drama between them. It was almost a miracle to see them all getting along, and it made it so much easier and more relaxing for Taryn to drive safely to their new home.

"We are going to be dynamite, everybody!" Taryn said. "Don't worry about a thing, all right? Everything will be A-OK, and if it isn't, then we can go back to blaming Dad for everything." Taryn tried her best to bring the family closer together with a little motivational attitude of her own.

Everything was looking pretty much back to normal with Taryn and her family for the time being. They all sat quietly and enjoyed what was left of Nicole's well-cut coke in their mysterious home in the town of Skank Hill.

CHAPTER 7

Family Home Cleaning

Back at the new Barstool family home, everybody stood speechless in the middle of the living room after tearing down all the two-by-fours that remained on the windows and doors of the house.

"You know what, you guys? This might not be such a bad house," Sanchez said. "It has so much more space than our old house, and it even smells better! Thanks to your sister, Lacy, it no longer has that washed-up pussy smell that the other house did! Sorry, Lacy, I had to put you on the spot, but you have been around the block more than enough times, so sometimes you can bring an awful smell to the house. For future reference, that might be something you need to work on—maybe go to the doctor and schedule a scrub-and-wash appointment or something. I don't know, but you got to think of something because you're not going to be smelling up this house like you did the last one."

Lacy felt so embarrassed and ashamed after her father laid down one of the first rules of the house for her. "This place already smelled like pussy. You are a fucking dirtbag; it used to be an old whorehouse!" Lacy yelled, but Sanchez paid no attention.

"Yes, you're right, darling. This house does smell like pussy, but the good kind of pussy—class-A pussy, like it was imported here from Russia! Now that's the good pussy. It always stays cold and fresh and tastes like grilled salmon. Mm-mm-mm!"

All Stanley could do was laugh as he stood there and watched his sister getting clowned on by their father, Sanchez. "Yeah, that's right; you tell her, Dad! Let that bitch know what pussy is all about!" Stanley shouted as he looked over at Lacy with a goofy smile.

"Shut the fuck up, Stanley! At least I'm getting some around here, unlike you! I heard you haven't got laid for almost ten years now. Is that true?"

Stanley could only stand there, stiff in his shoes, wishing she had never said that. "Lacy, you rotten old sister of mine! You were not supposed to tell anybody about that!"

"Aw, shut up, Stanley. The only ones who know are just us, your own goddamn family. I don't want to hear any of your sissy shit right now because I'm trying my best to settle into this new pussy shithole house, and I have you and Dad talking about pussy all day! In other words, Stanley, get the fuck out of my face! Go clean something! Or better yet, clean your fucking self! Starting with the back of your ass, and make sure you clean that real good because it fucking stinks! Goddamn it, Stanley, wash your fucking ass. Dad, please say something to him. That's your son. What's the matter with you?"

"Stanley! Now, you'd better listen to me, son! Your sister is right, so you'd better march your nasty ass into that bathroom and take a long shower before I grab you by your neck and hose you down! Go on, boy, now get! Vamoose!"

For poor Stanley, it just felt like the whole world was tumbling down on him again. "I can't believe my own family always turns against me. I did nothing wrong!"

Lacy felt she had no other choice but to continue complaining about Stanley's rude behavior to her father. "Dad! Stanley is having another one of his periods again!"

Once again, Sanchez raised his voice to Stanley, but he meant everything he said to him this time. "I have already told you, boy, and you didn't listen! I have no other choice but to take your monkey ass outside and hose you down myself. I will make sure you get scrubbed down the same way a guard would do it at a Mexican prison. And for your safety, I feel it would be best if you just sit still and don't move an inch because it will only make it harder for yourself."

Stanley was not a good fighter, so it didn't matter how hard he fought back. He was just no match against his father and his violent behavior.

Lacy could not help but laugh every time Stanley screamed like a little girl as Sanchez pulled him by the hair to the bathtub. "You'd better stop standing around laughing, Lacy! This was your idea, so you'd better give me a hand with this stinky son of a bitch," Sanchez said loudly.

Lacy refused. She didn't want to help because of how dirty Stanley was. "I'm not touching that nasty motherfucker, Dad! That's a father-and-son moment, so you deal with him. I will be too busy turning this nasty whorehouse into a lovely family home for all of us."

Lacy's words made Sanchez so angry that he felt he had no choice but to take the brown leather belt off his waist so he could beat the living shit out of Stanley, hoping it would make his job much easier.

"Dad, please, stop! I don't need your help. I will clean myself!" Stanley said.

But those crying words were not good enough to make his father, Sanchez, put down the belt. "No way, Stanley! You had that opportunity set up for you a long time ago, and you didn't take it, so now, here we are. You're the only one suffering, so don't you blame anybody else but yourself, boy! Now take that washrag and wash all the black off your ass!" Sanchez said as he continued to beat Stanley with the brown leather belt.

Stanley screamed in so much pain. "This is fucked up, Dad. You don't need to do this. What the fuck is wrong with you? You never did any crazy shit like this to Lacy or Pauley!"

Sanchez had an answer for everything at that moment. "That's because your sister is all paid off from personal sexual activity, and your brother, Pauley, is as gay as a fucking ghetto pit bull. You don't want one of those motherfuckers humping your leg. That's why I just sometimes stay as far away as I can from that faggot ass and hope that one day he will get lost in some woman's 'Virginia.' But you, Stanley, I have time for you. I'll always have time for you, so you'd better quit wasting my time with all your crying and bitching! You still have to take your bath, boy! Keep scrubbing that black off your ass, or I'll give you something to cry about!" Sanchez again beat Stanley down with the belt.

After about an hour of beating and scrubbing Stanley in the bathtub, Stanley's father, Sanchez, felt it was finally enough and decided to put the brown leather belt away and to kick Stanley out of the bathroom so that he could take a shit. "All right now, Stanley. I hope you learned yours. Listen, boy! You'd better start taking a shower every day. Now get the fuck out of the bathroom because I must take a shit like you would not believe."

Stanley was glad that his bathtub punishment was finally over, but there was still much work to be done around the new house, and he felt there was no reason he should help because of what just had happened.

"Are you going to help us fix this place up, Stanley, or will you just stand there dripping water all over the living room floor?" Lacy asked.

"Fuck you, bitch! You, the old man, and the rest of the family can fix it yourself! I'm going to pick out my room and not come out for the rest of the day!"

"Good, you little shit! Remember, though, that you get the smallest room because you're the fucking stank-ass sheep of the family, and you deserve nothing but the worst. You always will be on the bottom no matter what because you're a fucking cocksucker!"

Lacy's cruel words didn't mean anything to Stanley. He had been putting up with her shit for his entire life and could not have cared less for whatever came out of her mouth. "Don't worry about what room I pick out. If it were up to me, I would put you out in the backyard to live in a shaggy tent with your whore stepmother who you love so much."

Lacy never liked it when Stanley talked bad about their stepmother, Amelia. After their mother's death, it was hard for Lacy to get over it, and now, since their father had found someone new and got remarried, it was like having a new mother all over again, which meant a lot to her. "Don't talk about Amelia like that! She is our new mom, and you best show respect, or I'm going to get you good one day."

"No, you won't. Bitch, you are not going to do shit!" Stanley replied.

"I'll tell everybody your dark secrets, Stanley. I'll embarrass you so bad that you won't be able to step out of the house for at least a year! Even after that, it still wouldn't matter because they will still remember, and they will make fun of you for the rest of your worthless life."

Stanley would not back down; he continued to egg her on. "I have no dark secrets, bitch, so shut the fuck up before I backhand you a good one across the face!"

"That's it, Stanley! You just wait. I will tell everybody you know about your fat women's fantasy problem and how you like to stare at their feet because you have a disturbing foot fetish!"

"Oh no! You crazy fucking bitch, you said that you would never tell anybody that shit!"

"Well, then, don't make me tell anybody that crazy shit, Stanley. Help us out around the house."

Stanley then decided it would be best to just shut his mouth and help clean up the new house before his crazed sister, Lacy, did something that he would regret. "OK, I'll help out, but please don't tell anyone my dark secrets. I don't want anyone to know that shit."

After all that was said, there was no reason anymore for Lacy to humiliate Stanley.

Stanley held it together and helped everyone clean the house, just like he said he would.

CHAPTER 8

Skank Hill Arrival

After a long and tiring drive from Vegas, the moment that the Cherry family had been waiting for so patiently was finally right in front of their eyes—the town of Skank Hill. The town wasn't exactly what they had pictured in their minds, but Taryn and her father, Johnny, didn't care much. They were just so happy to arrive finally.

Nicole, on the other hand, had a different opinion. "Oh, my fucking God! Where in the fuck did this crazy old man take us? Maybe we're just stopping in this town to get gas or something. I know this fucking old man wouldn't leave us here to stay! This place looks like a real dump; not even an old, burned-out hooker would work these corners! I know; I have been doing this kind of work almost my whole life."

"Yes, you sure have, darling, because you're Daddy's little girl!" Johnny called out from the back seat of the car.

"Shut the fuck up, old man! Can't you see that there is a female bitch talking? And when there is a female talking, the man must know to shut the fuck up!" shouted Nicole.

"Relax, little sister," Taryn said. "We'll make everything work here as a family, just wait and see."

"Yes, I know. I just get frustrated when things don't go my way—and then I turn into a crazy bitch. I'm sorry; I don't mean no harm, you guys. My mental illness sometimes cannot help itself, but when I click my heels three times and do my breathing exercises, I feel so much better."

"Maybe you should start doing them now and quit your goddamn yapping, you stupid bitch!" Johnny said, with a big smile on his face.

"I thought I told you to shut the fuck up back there, you fucking jackass!"

Johnny didn't care because Old Man Peter was pulling up in the driveway of their brand-new home. "Look, you stupid bitches! We must be here!" Johnny shouted.

They all couldn't have been more excited. Being in that car, all together, had been driving them nuts. They pulled to the other side of the road because the driveway was small, and then they quickly got out to examine the house.

"All right now, Mr. Cherry, this is the only house I have available for you folks. It's yours if you want it; if not, then get the fuck out! See if I'll ever help you again!"

"Yeah! Yeah! We'll take it! Now, what about the other part of the business? How does that go?" Johnny asked.

"Oh yeah! You must mean the money part, huh? When will you pay me the first month's rent? Look here, Mr. Cherry, there are two ways we can do this. Either you can give me cash by the end of each month—let's say about $250 a month; I think you should be able to handle that—or, if you like, you can sell me one of your daughters for a good fun time behind the shed once a week, and you will never have to pay me a single dime. What do you say?"

"Well, it sounds like a good idea, but I still have to ask my daughters for their approval."

"Of course, sir, I wouldn't want to do business any other way, but I will need an answer soon. I'm not going to wait forever either, so I'll tell you what—I will give you three days, Johnny, and that's it. I'll need an answer by then. Now, you all enjoy your new lovely home, and I shall be back in three days."

As Johnny watched him drive slowly down the road, he still couldn't believe that they had scored such a great deal on the house in just a short time, and he couldn't wait to tell Taryn and Nicole about Peter's wonderful idea for rent payment arrangements. He was sure they would be so excited and jump for joy—but fathers don't know what's best as an everyday father-and-daughter moment. "Hey, you guys, guess what? Peter will give us one hell of a deal on this house if you two agree to suck his dick once a month—oh my God, wow! Look at this place. It's truly amazing!"

Taryn and Nicole had different opinions, and they could not wait to express what they thought. "Are you kidding us, Dad? This whole house smells like shit!" Nicole said. "Like rotten, used tampons and masturbation magazines! They even left all their shit behind for us to clean up, and it's not even good shit. It's all worthless! Not even a crooked salesman at a pawn shop would want anything to do with this shit."

Johnny didn't know what to say about their feelings for the house. He wasn't sure if it was the right time to bring up Peter's once-in-a-lifetime deal, but he knew it had to be done. "Oh, don't worry about the house," he told them. "Once we get settled in and make this place all nice and wonderful to our satisfaction, everything will be fine. But on the other hand, I was talking to Old Man Peter, and he has this great idea for how we can stay here rent-free!"

Normally, they would have been thrilled about living somewhere rent-free, but Taryn and Nicole showed no signs of jumping for joy because they already knew that Old Man Peter was up to no good, and they knew how stupid their father was. He might possibly have gotten them all involved in another scandalous mess.

"Oh no! What the fuck did you do this time, Dad?" Taryn asked.

"What the fuck do you mean? What did I do? I just scored us a rent-free deal with Old Man Peter! He said we can stay here as long as we want, as long as you two agree."

"Agree to what, Dad? What the fuck did you tell him?" Nicole shouted.

Just the sound of her voice made Johnny shiver in fear, but he knew he couldn't stay silent at that moment. He had to tell them everything. "You know how old people are—sometimes they have unique needs, and they can't help but express themselves in their elderly way. Therefore, Old Man Peter kind of had this great idea of allowing you two girls to fulfill his fantasy by showing him a good time once a month—maybe even twice, if it's not too much to ask—and that would be our payments for each month, no cash necessary! So what do you two think? Did your papa find us a good deal or what?"

Nicole was speechless, but Taryn was outraged. "You mean that would be our rent payment for the month? What the fuck are *you* going to contribute to this deal? Did you tell Old Man Peter that you would be willing to suck his balls? Maybe even stick your tongue down his mouth and give him a hand job simultaneously? I'm sure he would like that! Why the fuck would you tell him that we would even consider doing such a thing, you asshole?"

"Don't worry, OK? I told him I would have to ask you two first to ensure it was OK before closing the deal. But just so you know, time is a factor right now. I'm going to need an answer as soon as possible. He will also need a house payment as soon as possible. We don't have any cash to give him right now, so if you two don't want to go through with this, maybe you can think of a better idea to pay the rent because I'm out of ideas. Still, you two would have to think of something quick because he will be back in three days, expecting rent money or a dirty nasty blow job that I know you two do so well! So what's it going to be, my precious little daughters? Are you two down or what?"

Taryn always had been smarter than her dad, and she knew how to outsmart him in every kind of way. In this situation, she knew exactly what she was doing. "As I said before, Dad, you're going to have to contribute something to this deal too. Nicole and I will not let you sit on your ass while we do all the hard work for that dirty old man! You need to tell him that you'll show him a good time!"

Johnny knew exactly what Taryn was talking about, but he was unsure if he could go through with that. "I don't think Old Man Peter is in to guys. I'm sure that he only wants a woman to handle all his sexual needs."

Taryn wouldn't let him off that easily; she also had an answer for that. "Oh, don't you worry about that, Father. I'll talk to Old Man Peter myself when he arrives in three days. I'll tell him that you're also going to get in the mix of all this. I'm sure he will be super thrilled to know that you want to suck his dick as well; then he will have three times the fun! He might even buy us dinner every night after I renegotiate this deal. So now I ask you, Father: are you down or what?"

The tables had turned. Instead of Nicole being speechless, the sounds of silence were now absorbing every inch of Johnny from head to toe, and there was nothing he could do but continue to stand there looking stupid.

"What's the matter, Daddy-O? Cat got your tongue?" Nicole asked. "Did someone shit in your cereal again? You look a little pale, old man!

Did you have a bad dream of Rudolph the Red-Nosed Reindeer fucking your mother or something?"

Johnny still didn't have much to say about Nicole's disrespectful sense of humor. "That's your fucking grandma you're talking dirty about, you lowdown bitch! Show some goddamn respect; that's your grandma!"

Nicole showed no remorse and continued with her self-righteous ways. "Dad, shut the fuck up. Nobody here gives a fuck about being kind to Grandma, so stop acting like a little bitch! And don't try to weasel yourself out of this deal either! You started this shit, and now I'm finishing it! And if I say you have to suck that old man's dick, then goddamn it, you will suck that old man's dick, whether you like it or not!" Nicole said with a firmer voice.

"Oh, come on, guys, please! This isn't right. I shouldn't have to mix up with a guy. Can't you find me a ninety-year-old lady instead? I know I can put a big dent in that ass!"

"Sorry, old man, but we are a family, and we work as a team. That's something you need to learn. If I hear your voice one more time talking about how you don't want to go through with this, Taryn and I will kick you out of this place so quick you won't know what to do! And the way this town looks, you wouldn't last for one minute being homeless on the street. You'd better slow your roll with us—you got that, mister?"

There was no pulling out of this deal that Taryn and Nicole would soon rearrange, and Johnny knew he would have to follow up on every sexual activity that would need to be done. There wasn't a damn thing he could do about it but shed a few tears of sorrow.

"Don't just stand there and cry!" Nicole scolded. "Help us fix up this place. These people left us with much good shit that we can still use. Everything we don't want, we'll burn in the backyard. Why don't you make yourself useful and find some wood to make a huge bonfire. Taryn and I will pile up the shit we don't need, and you can take it out back for us. Do you think you can handle all that?"

Now that Johnny knew there was no way out of the tight situation that his daughters were about to put him in, he decided that maybe if he did everything they asked him to do and acted very polite at all times, they wouldn't force him to go down on Old Man Peter after all. And so he went throughout the rest of the day, acting as pleasant as he could be. "Well,

I guess you two are right. I shouldn't let you guys do all the hard work. I should contribute as well. Girls, I'm not getting any younger, and I wasn't sure if my health would be up for such a thing. My back these days is not the same as it used to be when I was your age, and I ain't kidding either. The older you get, the more your body slowly goes to shit."

Once again, Taryn and Nicole were one step ahead of their father. They knew that he was trying to weasel out of the rearranged deal. "Listen here, Dad! You ain't getting out of this!" Taryn said. "You're sucking some old man's cock whether you like it or not! Besides, old-man sex is best between two grown men. We can also make a porn video out of this to make a little side money. I could probably get that old fucker to invest in some cameras for this project. It will be no problem to get him to fork over some cash, Nicole and I can handle that, no sweat—well, maybe a little sweat, but after that, it's all you, Dad."

"You two are fucking nuts! Old Man Peter would never agree to do such a thing and never would give you two dollars for any porn movie either. Get that fantasy out of your heads now!" Johnny said.

"Of course that crazy old man will give us money for the cameras to make a porn movie! It's the fucking seventies; everybody these days is making a porn movie! It's the most popular thing, next to coke, and I bet you anything that dirty old man does it all."

Right then and there, Johnny decided that enough was enough. He was no longer going to be Mr. Nice Guy. "Man, fuck the both of you! You all ain't going to be the one talking to Peter because I'm going to talk to him, and he's not going to like the faggot porn you have in mind for me and him to do! He's going to say hell fucking no! Get the fuck out of here with that shit!"

Johnny's words did not scare Taryn and Nicole one bit. "You forget who's in charge of this situation, Dad, and it's not you!" Taryn said. "Women are the rulers of sex, and once Nicole gives him a little sample of some of our goods, your complaints won't mean a fucking thing to him! So you'd better find yourself a dildo to practice your dick sucking. A dildo is always best for mouth exercise. You don't have much time because three days is just around the corner, so get to sucking, bitch."

Johnny shook his head in anger. "We'll see who's right, bitch, when he arrives. I'm sure whether or not you two throw pussy in his face, he ain't going to have it in his stomach to want to do some queer shit like you all have planned in your sick fucking minds!"

"Don't you worry one hair on your head, Father. We'll find out soon enough what he thinks about our wonderful idea, and when he decides on our behalf, your ass will belong to us, and you fucking know it. There ain't shit you are going to do about it either but suck his fucking dick and shed tears down your pretty cheeks."

Once Taryn and Nicole got everything they needed to say off their chests, they decided it would be best to ignore their father for the rest of the day and continue working on fixing up their new home.

CHAPTER 9

Old Man Peter Returns

Three days had come and gone quickly for the Cherry family. As the sun rose on that particular morning, it felt like Christmas for everybody. As an ex-Marine, Johnny was the first to wake up, as usual. He also wanted to be the first one to talk to Old Man Peter—before Taryn and Nicole did. He knew they would say something that would jeopardize his heterosexual body. So now, as everybody continued to sleep throughout the house, Johnny stood by the window and waited as the coffee heated up on the stove.

"I'll make sure that Old Man Peter feels right at home with a nice cup of java when he gets here. That will make him more willing to decide on my deal, instead of what those bitches have to offer him," he whispered to himself.

But the smell of coffee burning in a cheap cracked floral pot would soon spoil Johnny's plans.

"Good morning, Father! Making coffee for all of us? Thank you so much, just what Nicole and I need. I sure hope that we have clean cups around here, or we might have to send you on a plastic-cup mission."

"That coffee is not for you guys; it's for Old Man Peter, so leave it alone!"

Taryn could not believe what she was hearing from her own father that morning. "Oh, so that's what you're trying to do, huh? You're trying to bribe him with this cheap-shit coffee to make him side with your deal over mine. You forget that Nicole and I have the pussy hypnotizer, and that will make your nice cup of java taste like a nice cup of shit! You'd better hold on to your pants, old man, because when he gets here, they coming off. Old Man Peter is going to be all up in your ass, and you will do nothing but take it like a champion, just like the rest of us, so get ready!"

Taryn and Nicole helped themselves to cups of coffee and left almost nothing for Old Man Peter.

"Goddamn it, you two nearly drank it all! Now what the fuck is he going to drink?"

As Johnny hurried to make another batch, he could hear Peter's loud-engine Chevy pulling up the driveway. "Oh, goddamn it, he's already here!" Johnny yelled. As he continued to warm up the coffeepot on the stove, he could already see Taryn and Nicole from the corner of his eye—they were walking out the front door to welcome him with sexual greetings.

"Hey baby, nice to see you again," Nicole said. "I was hoping you would show up earlier. I've had my mind on you for a while and can't wait to get my hands on you. Maybe you can take me and my sister, Taryn, for a ride in your little love machine, and we can show you a perfect time."

Old Man Peter was excited and filled with joy at hearing those naughty words from Nicole's mouth. As she softly moved her hands from his chest to the inside of his pants, he knew she was blessed with a great hand job experience.

"Damn, women, let's get in the car and go for a ride. I'll take you two anywhere!"

"Oh, Peter, do you mean that? Taryn and I have been working so hard, getting situated at the new house for the past three days, and we're just dying to get out and see the new town a little. If it's OK with you, I would sure like to drive this wonderful muscle machine you have here."

"Oh, I don't know about that, sweet cakes. I never let anybody drive this car. She's my baby, and I just couldn't let anything happen to her."

But Nicole wouldn't let him leave the driveway until she had her way. "But baby, I would be so much hornier if you let me drive it, and so would Taryn. If you let us drive it, we will let you drive us—and not only for today but anytime you want."

"Oh boy! Take the fucking keys, and let's get out of here. Come on, now! You two can't make an old man wait a day! I'm so glad you two decided to go through with the deal I talked to your father about a few days back."

Taryn knew she had to say something right away, just as Nicole backed out of the driveway and into the street. "Oh yeah, we heard about that deal too, and we have a few requests of our own to add to the contract, if you don't mind. We have a new arrangement deal that we've been working on, and we feel it will be perfect for all of us."

Old Man Peter wasn't sure what she meant by *new arrangement deal*, and he wanted to know more. "Hey, goddamn it, nobody told me nothing about any new arrangement deal. I sure as hell don't think I want to listen to it either!"

Nicole quickly had to make him feel like there was nothing to worry about. "Don't you worry now, baby. You're just going to love what we have in mind; it will blow you away."

Just as they peeled off into the street, Johnny finally made his way out the front door. "Hey, Peter, I made you some coffee!" But it was too late. Taryn and Nicole had already taken off before poor Johnny could even speak with him. "Goddamn it! Those two bitches fucked me over again. Just wait until I get my hands on them! I will make them go out and fetch me a switch off a tree, just like I used to when they were little. I'm going to beat their asses so black and blue that they won't be able to sit for a week! Then we will see who's laughing!"

It was a sad little moment for Johnny, and he knew that they were already blabbering away about their new arrangement, which he was not willing to go through with—not in a million years. And so, instead of waiting eagerly at home, he decided to jump into the Pinto and look for them. "I better find them before they convince Peter to go through with this crazy shit, and I sure can't let that happen! Not on my fucking watch; that's for damn sure!"

Poor Johnny always had the worst luck, and as he tried to leave the driveway, he realized right away that he was out of gas. "Fuck, man! I can never catch a fucking break!" he shouted. This time, he knew there was nothing else to do but stay home and wait for his two lousy daughters to come home with a gay, horny old man.

After a few minutes of waiting, he thought it would be best to go off on foot to look for all three of them so he could give them a piece of his mind.

"Fuck this shit! This town isn't all that big. I bet I can find them in a short time. I'll even take this baseball bat with me because when I see them, I will crack some heads wide open until they all see the deal my way!"

With a baseball bat in hand and without a single care in the world, Johnny went off down the road to explore the town of Skank Hill and to look for his two snotty daughters and a horny old man.

Meanwhile, Taryn and Nicole were still cruising down the road in Old Man Peter's hot rod on their little wild adventure. Peter decided to show them the ropes around the neighborhood and introduce them to everybody he knew. "Don't worry now, ladies. I'm going to show you two every inch of this town and let you know who's good people and who's not good people because if you don't know who you're getting involved with in this town, you could get yourself in a whole lot of trouble—perhaps even death, if you fuck up."

There wasn't one doubt in Taryn's and Nicole's heads at that moment that he was just talking out of his ass because by the tone of his voice, they knew he was for real. They just sat back as comfortably as they could and listened to every word the old man had to say.

"You see that fat redheaded woman standing down there at that corner, screaming at traffic? Her name is Kelly Burnout because she did so much acid and became perma-fried burned out. Her parents couldn't believe that their daughter had permanently fucked herself up, and they could not bear to look at her again. They no longer welcome her into their family home; they let her go journey by herself into the mean streets of Skank Hill."

"Wow, that's fucked up, old man. Who else do you know around here?" Taryn asked.

"I'm so glad you asked, my dear, because I know many more. You see that blind old man standing in his driveway with his Seeing Eye dog? His name is Ross. Nobody knows exactly how he became blind, but the rumor around town says he lost his left eye because he was spying on some teenage girls undressing in a locker room, and he lost his right eye in a BB gun fight. I guess they were playing some kind of war game; I don't know. But he does have a personal nurse who checks on him daily."

"Poor guy. I feel so sorry for him," Taryn replied.

"Oh, fuck him! He was an asshole anyway! But if you want me to show you a sorry son of a bitch, I will! You see that big white house, a couple of blocks down the street? That's an old whorehouse that's been a part of this town for many years, and the sorry-ass motherfuckers living in it are the ones that we kicked out of the place you live in now because they weren't paying their rent on time. They're the Barstool family, and they're a bunch of fuck-ups. Stupid fuckers!"

"Oh my, I feel so bad for their family. I wish that there was something we could do," Nicole said.

"Trust me; you don't want to help them! Their dad's a drunk, their stepmom's a whore, and the kids that live there don't have a shot at making it in this world! They will probably end up in jail or dead before twenty-one."

Sitting in the car and listening to Peter go on and on about how fucked up their family was made them think a lot about how fucked up their family was and how nice it was when someone went out of their way to show kindness from time to time. Even though Old Man Peter told them that the Barstool family was not worth helping, they still had intentions of helping anyway.

"You see that little piece of shit right there, picking his ass, thinking nobody is watching? His name is Stanley, the stupidest motherfucker in the Barstool family. Hell, he might even be the stupidest motherfucker in the town of Skank Hill! Or maybe even the state of Nevada. I got Stanley so drunk that he shit his pants, and then a bunch of friends and I made him walk butt naked all the way home. You should have seen the look on his poor face; it was hilarious. But he did it to himself. He knows he can't handle his liquor and shouldn't be drinking."

After hearing Old Man Peter ramble on and on about Stanley and his fucked-up family for so long, they finally grew tired.

"This was very nice of you to take us all around and show us the ropes around the town," Taryn said, "but I think it's best that you just take us home now. We're getting exhausted and need a nap."

Right away, Old Man Perter became very upset, knowing that Taryn and Nicole were no longer interested in his company. "Oh, come on, you two. You can't go home yet! What about our little business proposal that your dad and I talked about the other day?"

Taryn and Nicole looked at each other with a smile before they laid it down straight about how the deal would go down. "OK, first of all, I don't know what kind of fucking deal you and my father had together, but me and my lovely sister, Nicole, were not there to approve any of it. If you don't mind, we thought of a more suitable offer to make it more comfortable."

Peter looked very disappointed. He didn't want to hear what they had in mind, but because he hadn't had his dick wet in years, he knew it would be best to at least pretend that he cared if he wanted a shot at getting laid. "Oh, man! I thought I had this deal squared away, no questions asked. I guess I was wrong, so now, here we are, and I have to listen to this shit! So please, I beg you both, don't spoil my plans too much because I know that's what you're probably here to do. Is that correct?"

"Oh, relax, old man! It's not going to be all that bad. You're still going to get laid, just not by us."

"Oh, that's just great, you guys. I've been looking forward to this for the past three days! So you know what? Whatever you two are about to say, it better be good. I better hear you two say that you have a couple of chicks who are hotter than you guys put together and that they are both willing to suck my dick right fucking now!"

As mad as Peter was, all Taryn and Nicole could do was laugh and laugh, hoping that they would not piss their pants before they broke the news to him.

"I'm so sorry, Peter. We don't know any girls like that, but we do have someone else in mind who just might be suitable."

"Who the fuck is that?" Peter asked.

"Our father! He's not the best-looking man, but like the Bible says, a hole is a hole, even if it is the back of a man."

Peter was so confused that he almost ran out of words to say. "I never—with another man? That's just disgusting! Why would you two even consider that?"

"Hey, get over yourself, old man! Have you taken a look in the mirror lately? You're not exactly the best-looking man in Skank Hill; you know that?" Taryn yelled.

"Yeah, bitch, I know I'm not the best-looking man in town, but that doesn't mean I'm looking for dick action! You two just have a fucked-up way of thinking. If this is your way of trying to get out of paying rent, then you're wrong! The deal is cash or ass, and when I say *ass*, I don't mean your daddy's ass. I mean you guys' beautiful lush asses. Therefore, you two better put out or get the fuck out of town. I don't have time for this small-talk shit; you two got that?"

Taryn and Nicole's new deal arrangement wasn't working out the way they planned it, and to make things worse, their father, Johnny, showed up suddenly, out of nowhere, to inform Peter that he had nothing to do with their change of plans.

"Peter! Please, I beg you; don't listen to their words! I'm not down with any sick gay shit they have in mind, and you'd better not be, or I'll kick your ass myself!"

Peter was angry that Johnny would even think that he was gay, and he needed to let him know right away that he wasn't. "Do I look like somebody who would be into this sick gay shit? This was your fucking daughter's idea in the first place, asshole! Here I am, a man trying to help a good family get back on their feet, and this is how you all repay me! No, no, no! I can't do this anymore. I feel it's best that we just go our separate ways, and that starts with all you guys packing up your shit and getting the fuck out of that house! And not only that, I want you all out before the end of the night, and that's final!"

Johnny couldn't believe what his daughters had done. "Hey, you two, look what the fuck you did now! We had it made here, and all you two had to do was just suck an old man's dick from time to time—everything would have been fine! But no! You all had to fuck shit up! Thank you very much for everything I tried to do for you guys!"

Once again, Johnny was driving Taryn and Nicole up the wall with all his pissing and moaning, and they could not help but take their anger out on Old Man Peter himself for his "fucked-up ways," as they called it.

Old Man Peter slowly walked away toward his car with a smile. He failed to see Nicole come from behind with a cinder block in hand, which she had just stolen from a neighbor's front lawn, to shatter over his head. And like every great duo, they always backed up each other whenever needed. And that's exactly what Taryn did for Nicole.

With Old Man Peter lying unconscious on the street, Taryn needed to make sure he was truly dead. She quickly took the keys from his front coat pocket and jumped into his car as fast as possible. When she started up the engine, you could tell by the look in her eyes exactly what she had in mind.

Johnny was fired up now and could not believe his daughters would go this far. "Hey, you guys, what the fuck are you doing? Taryn, get the hell out of that car, you fucked-up bitch! Fun time is over! It's time to go home!"

But there was no way Taryn was going to listen to her father. With the engine roaring repeatedly, Taryn quickly threw the clutch into first gear and drove directly toward Peter's unconscious body lying peacefully on the street. "Die! You stupid piece of shit!" Those were Taryn's last words before the front tires on the car ran over Old Man Peter's head. To make things more amusing to her sick mind, she decided to continue her evil ways by reversing the car and driving back over his head. She just continued to run him over, again and again. Old Man Peter's blood was all over the street, and every bone in his neck was broken.

All the neighbors on the street did nothing but stand outside their front doorsteps and watch. Old Man Peter was not just a landlord for the Cherry family but many others around the town of Skank Hill. Everybody knew that Old Man Peter wasn't the best landlord, and so maybe just standing there, watching him die, was the best option for them.

Still, there is always one handy person in the crowd who's consistently generous. "You guys need help with the body? I have plenty of shovels and blankets!" one of the neighbors called out.

Taryn just waved him on. "No need for the help, sir! We have everything under control, but thanks anyway!"

So now, with nothing to worry about, they carried Old Man Peter's remains into his car and drove off as quickly as they could.

CHAPTER 10

Dead Fucking Landlord

After they left the crime scene, the girls felt like so much weight had been lifted off their shoulders, and they were happy and giddy inside for the first time since their mom died. But their father, Johnny, was not, and they once again had to hear out his worries and frustration.

"What the fuck, man? What the fucking fuck?" Johnny shouted with fear. "That shit was crazy, you guys! Pull this fucking car over, dump this body on the road, and get the hell out of this town!"

"Dad! Chill the fuck out! Taryn and I got this shit all right. We know what the fuck we're doing! We are not leaving Skank Hill because we have it made here, and you know it! This situation is not as horrible as it looks. All we have to do when we get home is bury the body and carry on with our lives. Nobody in this town will say shit because I'm going to do two things to keep them quiet: either fuck their brains out or bash their fucking heads open with a sledgehammer. But for right now, you need to chill the fuck out! You're acting like you never killed anybody. What the hell is the matter with you?"

Johnny knew he had not been a good father, and even though he knew there was nothing he could say to set their minds straight, he still tried. "Look here, you two fucking mistake children of mine—everybody I killed in Vietnam, including your mother after the war, is now all put behind me. I don't want you two repeating the same shit I did because it's not worth it! It will give you horrible nightmares for the rest of your life, and I don't want the same for you guys."

Taryn and Nicole didn't overthink their father's words. As they looked at each other with a smile, they knew it was their turn to set him straight. "Oh, stop it, Dad!" Taryn said. "You acted like you had to do time for your wicked crimes, but you never did. And don't talk to us about nightmares because, as we have discussed before, you were the one who gave us chronic nightmares when you killed Mom in front of us! So now, let's just stop arguing and help each other out as a family."

During everything that was going on at that moment, Johnny knew that was the best thing they could possibly do. As far as getting rid of the body, Johnny knew exactly what to do. He was an expert at getting rid of dead bodies because of his wild experiences, and he felt it was his duty to instruct his two daughters on hits done professionally. "You guys are ready. We need to work together as a family team and get shit done. Now, don't you two worry about Old Man Peter's body because I know exactly what to do. I have done this shit plenty of times before in my lifetime, so just sit back and let the pro show you how it's done."

As soon as they got home, Taryn and Nicole were excited and could not wait to dispose of the body, but to their father, Johnny, it was no picnic.

He had to inform them that it could sometimes be a very messy job. "OK, you two, let's get down to business. Remember that whatever I say to do, just do it, and there will be no problem."

For most of their lives, the girls had never listened to a single word their father said because he was always such a drunken mess, but this time, they knew that it was crucial to hear him out.

"You got it, Dad! Nicole and I will do whatever you want. Don't worry; we have your back."

At first, Johnny was amazed that Taryn and Nicole were finally paying attention. It was like music to his ears, hearing his daughters tell him that, and he couldn't wait to get started. "All right, you guys! First, we have to carry this motherfucker into the house without anybody seeing us. I know it seems like nobody in this town cares about cold-blooded murders, but we still have to be careful and be quick. It won't take long before his body starts smelling up the house."

Without saying a word to their father, Taryn and Nicole looked at each other with frustration. "So why the fuck is he making us take the body in the house in the first place, if it's going to do nothing but stink up the house?" Nicole asked.

"I don't know, baby sister, but if we just do what he tells us, this will all be over before we know it."

It wasn't a worrying situation for Taryn and Nicole; it was more like an adventure or some kind of field trip for them. They were so excited to be a part of the moment and could not wait to get their hands dirty from all the blood dripping from his body in the back seat of the car.

"OK, Nicole, you take one end, and I'll take the other and just bring Old Man Peter into Dad's room."

"Don't take that fucking thing into my room! I don't want it smelling up the place! I have to sleep there, goddamn it!"

All Johnny's pissing and yelling did nothing but drive Taryn completely nuts. "Well, we can't leave the old man in the fucking living room either! You stupid fuck! This is the family room, and it should be cozy and pretty and smell like a wonderful blooming flower, not like a stinking, fucking, dick-licking, dirty old man's corpse!"

"All right, bitch. I get it! Just bring him into the kitchen, and I'll take care of the rest by myself! I don't need you guys' help after that because you're just going to drive me crazy!"

Still, it wasn't good enough for Taryn's satisfaction. "Don't bring him into the fucking kitchen either, you idiot! We have to prepare our meals there, and we can't have that old man stinking it up!"

"Jesus fucking Christ, woman! It never fucking ends with you, does it?" Johnny said.

Taryn wasn't quite through yet. "You told us both that you knew how to get rid of this fucking body, and now it looks as if you don't even know what the fuck you're doing! So you need to figure your shit out, dude. Get your fucking head right or something! Because we have a major family crisis on our hands!"

"The only reason we're in this fucking jam is that your crazy-ass ran him over with the car. And now I'm cleaning up all the fucking dirty work! So please, please don't question me anymore about how I'm handling the situation you got us all into! Because like I said before, I don't need your guys' help. I can do this shit by myself!"

Still, Taryn was not satisfied. "Sorry, Dad, but we're not letting you off that easy! We are a family and will come together and handle this crazy shit together."

Johnny knew he had no choice; he was stuck working with them. From that point on, everything got a little more frustrating for him, and he had to just deal with it.

"First of all, Dad, we need to stick this old man up in an attic for a little while so we can dig a big hole in the backyard. When we're done doing that, we can drag him back out and put him into the fucking ground where he belongs!"

Even though his daughter was calling the shots, Johnny still thought it would be funny to question her intelligence. "Don't you think it would be easier just to throw him down the basement, dumbass? Or maybe bury him out in the desert—like everybody else does?"

"Look here, you stupid fuck! There is no basement in this house. As a matter of fact, you won't see many basements in any home in the state of Nevada because they're too hard to dig out here! Your little desert plan would have been a good idea if you had brought that up before we came back to the house, you fucking dumbass! Now, don't question me anymore about how I'm running shit! I thought you were a man who knew what he was doing, but obviously, you're not! So here we are, your innocent little daughters, who have to help their father dispose of an old beat-up corpse. Man, I swear, you're fucking worthless!"

Johnny didn't feel like fighting with his daughter Taryn, but he needed to. "Your mother used to call me worthless. I never liked it when she called me worthless, so you'd better watch your step with me, bitch! Or I'll pop your fucking lip open and make your baby sister lick your blood off the ground. You both disgust me and remind me of your whore mother every day! Sometimes, there were things she said that made me very angry! And it was just too hard for me to handle, so I had no choice but to fix the problem. I'm just warning you two right now—don't call me worthless anymore, or I'll fix you! I didn't have anything to do with the mess you two caused tonight. I liked the old man, but you just ran him over! So what I'm going to do right now is just take a nap. And when I wake in the morning, he better be six feet under, or you two will be six feet under!"

Taryn decided to say nothing and just let her father walk away. She knew he was right in his soft of fucked-up way, so she had to give him credit for that.

Nicole, on the other hand, begged to differ. "What are you doing, Taryn, just letting Dad walk away like that? Fucking say something to him, man, because we can't do this ourselves." She then shouted at her father. "Hey, asshole! Are you going to help us or what?"

Taryn could only try her very best to chill her out. "Just let him be, Nicole; just let it be."

"No, fuck that, He needs to get his ass back here and help us clean up this fucking mess like a goddamn family! Piece of shit! His mother is a fucking billy goat, and everybody fucks her!"

Taryn continued to do her best. "His mother is our grandma, you idiot! Why the fuck would you say that?"

"Look, goddamn it! I'm under much stress, so I don't want to deal with all this shit now. Don't worry! This won't take that long, and I'll do most of the work myself."

Finally, Nicole began to feel some relief. "Good! Because I don't feel like getting my hands all bloody. I can't break a nail right now. I have an appointment to get my nails done soon."

Taryn knew that Nicole wouldn't be a big help, so she decided to do everything herself because Nicole would be in the way. "You know, baby sister, I have a much better idea. Why don't you just run off and find us some dinner tonight, and I'll take care of everything here."

Nicole was so relieved to hear those words that she jumped for joy and kissed Taryn right on the lips. "Thank you, Taryn! You're the best sister anybody could ever have! And don't worry; I'll bring us back the best damn dinner any family has ever eaten!"

Taryn could only imagine what kind of dinner Nicole would bring home this time. The last time she was left in charge of dinner, she brought back roadkill possum and a few Tootsie Rolls. But this time, it didn't matter; Taryn needed to get Nicole out of the house so she could stay focused on the dead-body situation. Having Nicole around just made Taryn angry and too frustrated to think of anything.

Deep inside, Taryn was so tired and didn't feel like putting in any more hard work because she could only take so much. And so, without putting much thought into it, she decided to just drag him back out to his car, throw his body in the trunk, and ditch his vehicle somewhere on a lonely desert highway. *You know what? I'm not going to dig any fucking hole in the backyard*, she thought. *It would be easier to throw him in the trunk of his precious car and drive him somewhere far, far away.* She had no other idea. *That's the only thing I can think of.* "Come on, Old Man Peter," she muttered. "Back to the car you go before you smell the fucking house up! It's already bad enough that this place smells like ass and lonely dick misery."

Taryn was a strong young lady, so she toughed it out without saying another word and began dragging Old Man Peter's body back to the car to finalize his disappearance. During her hard work, without anybody's help, her mind developed new ideas for rules and structure to hold the family together so that they would not fail as a family, as they had done many times before. "Since I do so much work for this family, I think it's fair to make me the leader of this tribe," she said to herself as she loaded Peter's body into the trunk. "I'm the only one who gets her hands dirty in tight situations, so I'll be making my own set of rules for this family as soon as I get back from taking care of this shit!"

She didn't have a particular location in mind as to where she would dispose of his remains, just as long as it was far, far away. But her idea of *far away* was only seven miles down the highway, just outside the town of Skank Hill from where they'd entered. "This should be far enough. I'm not going to waste any more time on this old pervert. He doesn't even have enough gas in his fucking car to make it farther down the road." Time was going by quickly, and the sun began to set. Leaving the car on the side of the desert highway was all she'd come to do. "Wonderful! My job here is done, and now all I have to do is hitchhike my ass back to town. Hopefully, I'll get picked up by some horny drifter dude, so I can just suck him off for a ride home. That would be so lovely."

It usually didn't take long for a woman to hitch a ride back home, but it was like watching a comedy sitcom for Taryn. It was too bad she didn't have a mirror or even a perfume bottle because she looked like shit from all the hard labor and smelled like the corpse in the trunk. She only expected to wait for half an hour, tops, but she made it home on foot three hours later.

"I don't believe that there was not one motherfucker with the good-hearted generosity to give a bitch a ride home! It's times like today that I'm such a bitch to everybody who comes around! If life doesn't get any better anytime soon, I just might have to shoot myself, and if Nicole didn't pick up dinner, I'm going to shoot her!"

Being angry at that moment was all she could be, and taking it out on the family was the next thing on her mind, and she had no problem doing it. After everything she had been through, she felt she had the right, and the family deserved the lecture. "OK! Family fucking meeting! Right fucking now!"

The sound of her voice was like nails across a chalkboard, and Nicole and Johnny right away knew they were in for it but didn't know why.

"OK, Taryn! What the fuck is up? I brought home dinner, so why are you acting all nuts?" Nicole asked, holding a loaf of bread and a can of sardines.

"Hey, Taryn, what did you do with the body? Did you bury it, as I said?" Johnny asked with a smile on his face.

"Shut the fuck up, old man, before I make you join your wife in hell! And you, bitch! Come here!" Taryn looked straight into Nicole's eyes like a hawk on a squirrel.

Once again, Nicole had no idea what she was in for, and as she slowly made her way toward her sister, her heart began to beat rapidly. "Here you go, big sister. Have some sardine sandwiches. They sure are good."

Taryn wanted to lay down a good, honest lecture to her family at that very moment, but on second thought, she felt it would be best to contribute discipline instead to fulfill her immoral emotions. "Fuck your fucking sandwiches, bitch!" she shouted, slapping the sardine sandwiches out of Nicole's hand. "Now pick it up, bitch! Before I fucking slap you around!"

"Jesus fucking Christ, Taryn! What the fuck is your problem?"

Taryn was not satisfied with her response, so she continued the discipline. "I don't like sardine sandwiches, bitch! That's my fucking problem!" This time, she came from behind Nicole, grabbed her by the back of the neck, and rubbed her nose into the sardine sandwiches, which splattered all over the kitchen floor. "I'm not going to lecture you, bitch, so don't worry about that. I'm only doing this because it sexually excites me to see my baby sister cry like a little bitch! I don't remember who cries like a pussy more—you or Mom."

Johnny had heard enough. "Now you watch it, young lady, how you talk about your mama! She is up in heaven, watching over us! Show some damn respect!"

There was no way Taryn would allow her father to rain on her parade. "Didn't I tell you earlier to shut the fuck up, old man? And what do you know about respect, anyway? You're the one who put Mom up in heaven, so please don't share any poor nice-dad shit! Fuck you all! I'm the one holding this whole fucking family together! From now on, things will be run my way, whether you two like it or not. We are going clean this whole house up and make it smell nice and pretty. And when we are done with that, we will make peace with our neighbors and start acting like a real family around here!"

Suddenly, the smiles on their faces were gone, and they knew they had to start taking life much more seriously. Without dishing out feedback to Taryn's words, they decided to come together as a family to help make everything right.

CHAPTER 11

Wake 'n' Bake Morning

It wasn't hard for any of the Cherry family to get sleep that night. After everything they had been through, they were utterly exhausted and could not wait to rest their bodies on a soft-sheet bed. Before Taryn shut her eyes that night, she promised herself that she would go out and chat with the neighbors the next day, and Stanley Barstool would be first on her list.

After hearing Old Man Peter talk so severely about Stanley and his family, Taryn felt a little sorry for him and thought it would be an excellent idea to reach out and let him know that they were loving neighbors and nearby, if Stanley and his family ever need them.

"Good morning, Nicole!" Taryn greeted her sister the next morning. "Don't worry; I got coffee heating on the stove. You know, Nicole, I thought that maybe we should walk over to the Barstool family's house and say hi to Stanley."

"That sorry-ass piece of shit? Why would you want to waste your time on him? Besides, you heard what Old Man Peter said about him—his family's fucked up! And Stanley's the most fucked-up one of all. I don't know, Taryn. I think that guy is up to no good. Maybe you shouldn't bother him."

Taryn knew that it was a waste of time to encourage Nicole to understand how wonderful it was to show a little kindness to others. She didn't speak another word about it because, on second thought, she decided that it might not be a good idea to introduce Stanley to her sister. "Well, kid sister, what are your plans for today? Are you going to go out and get your nails done? Explore the town a little? Or maybe you and Dad should get together and clean this whole fucking house. I'm happy to share this morning joint with you, but you and Dad better start cleaning because you're the ass monkeys who mess it up the most."

Nicole couldn't disagree with a thing Taryn said because most of it was true. As she slowly touched her lips to the morning joint and took a puff, her thoughts of suicide and raping the next-door neighbor's cat went away. "No problem, big sister. I got your back. You can always count on me when you need something done, and when Dad wakes his ass up, I'm going to set him straight too."

Taryn was so proud of her kid sister for stepping up to the plate when the family needed it the most—not that Nicole hadn't stepped up to the plate before. She had prostituted herself plenty of times for the family to make the rent. But this time, it was different; it wasn't for sex or money. It was about finally doing something from the bottom of her heart, and Taryn just knew, from that moment, that anybody could change their reckless ways.

"Well then, little sister, I leave this house to you, trusting and hoping that you and Father will make the best of it. I'll be on my merry way to help a lost soul who needs some peace and harmony."

Nicole just scoffed and assumed that Taryn was talking about the same guy she was thinking of in her stoned-out little mind. "Who's the lost soul? Is it that stupid fucking Stanley bastard?"

"Yes! It's that stupid fucking Stanley bastard. We will have to get to know everybody in this town, sooner or later—that's how small it is. I know one thing, however. Every time I reach out and help somebody, the good Lord helps me right back." Taryn only hoped that Nicole would one day follow her generous ways, but that day wasn't today. So she said her last goodbyes to her dear sister and headed straight out the front door.

The smell of the fresh air brought a smile to Taryn's face as she stood on the front porch steps. "Umm, it's a beautiful day today, and I feel wonderful! I think I'll even bring my radio for this trip and sing along to Stanley's house. I hope he doesn't mind some stranger dropping by to say hello. We are new neighbors, after all. We all should get to know each other. Besides, it should be him welcoming our family into the neighborhood, but because he hasn't done that yet, I feel it's my duty, as a generous person, to do the right thing."

Taryn didn't care whether she was welcome there or not because she knew how men's minds worked very well, which made it very easy for her to control them. "I don't think Stanley is as bad as Old Man Peter made him out to be. Even if he is, I know how to handle it."

After just a few minutes of walking down the road, she finally arrived at Stanley's house. "Here we are," Taryn said quietly to herself as she slowly made her way up the porch steps. "Hello! Is anybody home?" she yelled.

No one came to the door, so she decided to give a little friendly shave-and-a-haircut knock to see if that would grab attention. It did, and before she knew it, a strange young man whom she recognized was at the door.

"Hi, I'm Taryn. My family just moved here, and I would like to take a moment to introduce myself to you as one of your newest neighbors."

Stanley was shy and speechless. He didn't know what to say. No girls ever talked to him or wanted anything to do with him.

"You must be Stanley. Old Man Peter has told me a lot about you. Can I ... come in?"

Standing nervously, still not knowing exactly what to say, Stanley decided to let her in. "Sure, yeah, come right on in." The thought that a sexy-ass woman was standing in his living room was all Stanley could think about. But he also had to keep in mind that his sister, Lacy, was sleeping in her bedroom. If she woke up and saw him alone with a beautiful woman, he knew she would most likely embarrass him right in front of her, as she had done with so many women, many times before.

Lacy never gave a flying fuck about her little brother, Stanley. She loved fucking up his life, and she would do it every time she had a chance. Stanley knew it, too, and that was why he decided right then and there that he needed to cut the visit short with Taryn and send her on her way home—before his fucked-up sister woke up and walked into the living room to embarrass him once again.

"You know what, Taryn? I just remembered that I don't have time to talk now because I have to help my dad fix the car. His dumb ass hit a deer one night, driving home drunk. The impact was so bad that it blew out the engine in the car, and now we don't have anything to drive. So that's why I must send you on your way—so I can help him fix the car. I don't mean to sound rude, but it's the dead truth."

Stanley was never a good liar; Taryn knew that right away. "Don't fuck with me, Stanley. I know when somebody is lying! You're just shy because I bet you never had a woman in your living room."

Stanley couldn't let her know that, so he continued trying to cover the guilt. "Yeah, right! I've had plenty of women before, baby! You don't know my dark side yet." Stanley had no clue how much of an idiot he was making of himself, but he did not care. He continued to make an ass of himself a little more. "You can ask any chick in the town of Skank Hill about me, and they will tell you I'm the best they ever had!"

Taryn was trying to keep from laughing because she knew Stanley was full of shit, yet he sounded serious about his story.

To make matters worse for Stanley and his idiotic lies, he heard his sister's squeaky bedroom door slowly open. He knew this wouldn't be good, so he had to prepare himself for whatever she would do.

"Well, look at this! Stanley, what are you doing? Don't you know this woman is too good for you? Quit wasting your time with this loser brother of mine! There isn't one bitch in this town who would want to touch him. He's a drunk, and he doesn't shower! Besides, he wouldn't even know where to stick it, even if he had the chance. Isn't that right, Stanley? You don't want someone like my brother Stanley. He used to get beat up all the time at school, and he doesn't even have a job! Do you want to know some more about him? He constantly masturbates to his favorite TV show, *Gidget*! He just can't get enough of that sexy Sally Field, can you, Stanley? His masturbation problem has gotten so bad that our dad has even caught him jacking off to old-lady cookbooks in the bathroom! He also has a small dick, and his nasty fucking feet stink! When was the last time you changed your underwear, Stanley? Didn't Dad tell you to change them a week ago?"

Stanley couldn't have felt any more embarrassed. He wanted to stand up for himself so badly and tell Taryn that his sister was nothing but a deceiving bitch and that everything she was saying was a lie. But he knew that wouldn't matter because his sister was so good at making a lie seem true and disturbing. "I'm so sorry, Taryn, but I have to go now. I hope you can find your way home by yourself," Stanley cried as he ran off to his bedroom, feeling ashamed and dripping with tears.

Taryn couldn't help but feel completely sorry for Stanley. She knew she had to stand up for him because Stanley wasn't brave enough to stand up for himself against his mean, rotten sister, Lacy. "That wasn't very nice to do to Stanley! Why would you even think about doing something so cruel to your brother?" Taryn shouted in a rage.

"Because fuck him—that's why," Lacy snarled. She felt she never needed to explain herself about Stanley, and so she always kept it short and sweet. "Where did Stanley find you, anyhow? He hasn't brought home a stray dog in a very long time, and when he did, I ran that bitch over with my car."

Taryn's first impression of the Barstool family home was not exactly going as she had wanted it to be. She had to make her peace with Lacy before she headed out the front door. "My name is Taryn. I just moved here with my family from Texas, and I'm just trying my best to make my acquaintance with everybody here in Skank Hill."

"Thank you very much, Karen, or whatever your fucking name is, but we have chores to do around here, if you can tell. And right now is not the best time for company. Even if you are new to this neighborhood, I don't give a shit! Maybe you should come back another day—like next week or something—because I'll be busting Stanley's ass around here until he understands the true meaning of a clean family home! Isn't that right, Stanley?" Lacy said with a smile, hoping that Stanley could hear her through his bedroom walls.

Taryn knew she would be back sooner than a week to check up on poor Stanley. "Very well, then. I'll be back in a week. Have a wonderful day."

Lacy never said another word; she stood there with a silly grin and watched Taryn walk out. She had already figured that Taryn most likely wouldn't return, and things would just go back to normal. "Stanley! You can come out of your room now! Your bitch went home and left without you!"

Stanley was so angry when he stepped out of his room. Every time he got so close to getting a girl to like him just a little bit, his sister always came in the middle of it and fucked it all up. "You stupid fucking bitch! Why do you always have to treat me like some piece of shit? I'm your brother; you're supposed to love me!"

Lacy could never stand listening to Stanley bitch about his emotional problems. She always thought he sounded like a whining little school bitch with his period. "Oh, shut the fuck up, Stanley! You're a loser, and everybody knows it, including your new little friend. Do you think someone like that would like you, Stanley? You're just a joke, and nobody thinks you're cool because you're the most worthless piece of shit in this town! You're never going to find happiness, Stanley, because you don't deserve happiness. You're a scumbag, and you like to suck big dicks, don't you, Stanley?"

Once again, all Stanley could do was just stand there stiffly and not do anything because he was too scared to stand up for himself. But deep down inside, he wanted his sister dead and chopped up into many pieces.

CHAPTER 12

Fucked-Up Sister

It was another night in the town of Skank Hill for the Cherry family in their new ramshackle home, and all Taryn did was gossip to Nicole about her trip to Stanley's house. "OK, girl, check this out. Stanley's sister is so fucked up; I mean, you are too but not as bad as Stanley's sister. You are like a fucking angel compared to Stanley's sister. But anyway, I felt pretty bad for the little bastard. He has to live in that rotten whorehouse with that fucked-up sister! His brain must be traumatized from dealing with all those cruel things she says about him. I haven't met the rest of the family yet, but I hope they are not like his sister because she is an absolute handful."

Nicole didn't give much thought to Stanley or his family, but she felt she needed to drop some sister-to-sister advice. "Now you listen up, Taryn. Don't go feeling sorry for Stanley just because he's mistreated a little bit around the house. That family sounds like trouble, and I don't think you should get involved with them! Besides, you said he was a little weird anyway, so why the fuck do you want to jump on his dick?"

Taryn stood against the wall with a smile on her face, and her eyes softly closed as she replied, "Oh, Nicole, if you could only see what I can see through these eyes. Stanley isn't as bad as his sister makes him out to be. I know that Stanley is a wonderful guy underneath it all. He sure could use a shave and a haircut and maybe even some modern clothes, but other than that, he's fine! I have doctored up plenty of men to my liking. Trust me when I say that Stanley won't be too much to change."

Nicole had her doubts. "I don't know, Taryn, but I'll tell you what! Maybe if you don't want me to worry, you should bring me with you next time so that I can meet the little fucker and make sure he's not some maniac."

Taryn couldn't help but smirk and scoff at her sister's remark. "Oh, come on, Nicole! He can't be any bigger of a nutcase than we are, and you know it!"

"I don't fucking care, Taryn. Either you bring me with you tomorrow, or I'll always keep bugging you about this."

Taryn had no problem with introducing her kid sister to her new friend Stanley; she was more than happy to do it. "All right. We'll go first thing tomorrow morning. I think you're going to like Stanley, and after that, you'll see how much of a sweet guy he is."

Nicole was excited to hear that her sister was willing to take her to Stanley's. "All right! Off to the ball, we go! Do you think I should wear one of my sexy dresses for his father? I wouldn't mind getting a little piece of ass while I'm out there."

"Oh my God, bitch! Chill the fuck out! I haven't even met the rest of the family yet, other than his sister, but she doesn't count. So just dress normally, please. This is no fucking disco nightclub."

Taking a trip to Stanley's house would be like a picnic for Nicole. She couldn't care less about her sister's feelings for Stanley. "Bitch, it's my disco nightclub! And if I want to wear a sexy party dress for all the guys to look at me—so they can come in their pants when I walk in the door—I'm going to do that!"

Johnny could hear his two daughters arguing downstairs from his bedroom. "That's right, Nicole! Don't take her shit! You wear that sexy dress! You sometimes remind me of your dead fucking mother when you wear dresses like that!" Johnny yelled at the top of his lungs as he slowly began jerking off.

"Shut the fuck up, Dad! Before I come and beat your fucking ass!" Nicole shouted.

All her father did was ignore her bad-tempered ways and continue jerking off. "Oh, shut up, Nicole. You're daddy's little girl. You're Daddy's little girl …" he said softly to himself as he slowly came onto the palm of his hand and drifted off to sleep.

Meanwhile, back at the Barstool family home, Stanley sat with his family in the living room, eating stale popcorn and watching *Gidget* on their ten-inch television.

"Why are you watching this stupid fucking show, Dad? This is Stanley's favorite show! It sucks! Turn off this shit!" Lacy yelled.

Her father, Sanchez, didn't want to hear it. "Oh, stop it now! You always watch what you want. Let Stanley watch what he wants for a change."

Lacy wanted to punch her dad in the nose for not agreeing with her, but instead, she just rolled her eyes and let Stanley have his way. "Fine, whatever. Let Stanley watch what he wants. He would never score with Gidget anyway because his dick is too small! He might even turn into a fit—ha-ha-ha-ha!"

Pauley had to defend himself from Lacy's rude remark. "You'd better stop it now, Lacy! You know damn well there is nothing wrong with being gay! I enjoy every minute of it!" Pauley said.

Lacy had to put her two cents in. "Yah, I'll bet you do like every minute of it—every minute of sucking big fucking dick! Ha-ha!" Lacy had the whole family laughing and in tears.

Even Pauley thought it was funny. "Yeah! You're right on that one, sis. I sure do like sucking some big dick from time to time, but not always. It's because it gives me throat burn, and then I have to eat cough drops for the whole day to cool it down."

Sanchez did not want to hear any more. "OK, there, Pauley, that was a little more information than I needed. You will not talk about your gay moments around me anymore. And Stanley, you'd better pay attention to your brother. You're already fucked up as it is, and if you don't get your shit together, you may become a queer too—just like your brother!"

"He already is, Dad," Lacy said.

"You'd better not be, Stanley, or I'll kick your fucking ass right now!" Sanchez said. "Get up!"

Lacy continued the vicious lies as she cheered her father on. "Yeah, that's right, Dad. Kick Stanley's fucking ass! I also heard him talking shit behind your back, saying he can beat your ass any time of the day!"

A fistfight between Stanley and his father, Sanchez, was a pretty common thing in their family, at least once a day. Still, not one fight had

75

ever gone in Stanley's favor. He always had to take an ass-kicking, and sometimes, the rest of the family would join in because it made them feel good to take pleasure in Stanley's misery.

"You'd better not be talking shit behind my back, Stanley! I'm your goddamn father, boy! You wouldn't even be breathing on this fucking earth if it wasn't for me. Just get the hell out of here before I beat the living shit out of you. Nobody here wants to watch your stupid fucking *Gidget* show anyway, Stanley, because it's an old show. Maybe you should watch *Three's Company* instead, like the rest of the world. Now, that's a great show! That fucking Jack Tripper—you never know what he's going to do next. Ha-ha! But anyway, Stanley, seriously, get the fuck out of here, and go to your room before we all beat the shit out of you!"

And so he did. Stanley had no choice but to do what his father told him to do. With his head hanging low and a sad face, he slowly made his way to his room, wishing he wasn't stuck in a dumpy house with a rotten family.

"You think he's in his room crying? I bet he's in his room crying right now," Lacy said.

The others paid no attention because they were too occupied, watching *Three's Company*.

"No, he ain't crying, but I bet you he's taking that needle to his arm again," Sanchez said. "Sometimes when that boy gets angry and frustrated, he likes to beat himself up with that skag junk shit! I swear that boy is going nowhere in life, and he will kill himself, just like his dead whore mother!"

Lacy couldn't help but laugh at her father's statement. "But Daddy, Mother never had a problem with drugs! It was your drinking and all your fucked-up ways that drove Mom to suicide."

Sanchez was sick and tired of being interrupted while watching his TV and did not want to hear anymore. "Look! Whatever Stanley wants to do in his personal life, he can do! If he wants to slam heroin, let that little motherfucker slam some heroin. I don't care anymore. Now shut up and let me watch my damn *Three's Company*!"

After that, Sanchez didn't have to say another word to Lacy or Pauley; they just smiled and watched the rest of *Three's Company* with their loving father.

While they were in the living room, Stanley was all alone in his room, and that was a whole new world. Stanley didn't have much to his name; his room only had a few things—a bed, a desk, a record player, sexy pictures of Sally Field taped on his wall, and a squeaky rocking chair where he would rock back and forth to ease his stress and pain from his family. It wasn't easy living with his family, and he had the track marks on his arms to prove it.

"I hate this fucking family so much," he said softly to himself, with tears running down his face. "I wish I'd been born into a family who gives a fuck about me, but I guess I wasn't born that lucky. All I have in this world is just myself and my fucked-up family! That's OK because I know how to make life just a little better. That's right! I know how to make life just a little ... better ..." Stanley cried as he slowly removed a dirty syringe from his long tube sock to draw up another fix for himself. "This fix here is for another miserable day on earth and for every junkie who can't afford it and is forced to settle for rehab!" Stanley slowly pierced the syringe into his left arm, like he had done many times before. "Uh ... yeah! That is much better. Let God's love run through my veins so I can preach his Word to all the world's wonderful people."

Stanley felt amazingly tremendous and wanted nothing more than to lie in his bed and pretend he was somebody else. At least that way, he could enjoy his fix in a more superior state of mind for another distressing period.

Throughout the rest of the night in the Barstool family household, Sanchez, Lacy, and Pauley continued to sit in the living room together and watch their family show, *Three's Company*, as Stanley lay in bed by himself, high as fuck and listening to his rock records as loud as he could.

CHAPTER 13

Taryn and Stanley

It was a rough night for both families, but they made it through and awoke the next morning. Nicole was the first to wake up because she was so eager to meet Taryn's new stupid friend—Taryn had bragged about him all night.

"OK, Taryn! Time to get up!" Nicole yelled as she pulled the curtains to the side to allow the sun to shine through the window.

Taryn pulled the covers over her head. "What the fuck, bitch? Go back to bed!" Taryn said wearily.

"Yeah, I know, I'm always waking you up so bright and early for something so stupid, but that's your fault! You should have never bragged last night about how cool you think that stupid fucking Stanley is. Now you got me excited and wanting to meet him too. So come on—get out of bed and get into the shower. I'll have a nice fatty rolled up for you by the time you get out. Sound good?"

Taryn did like the sound of that, but she knew she needed to haggle a little more. "Put some coffee on the stove top, and this bitch will wake up giddy and lustful."

Nicole was pleased that her request was not asking for too much. "You silly girl. You should have bargained a little better than that. I was already going to make coffee."

Even though Taryn didn't feel like moving one inch off the bed, she kept her word to her annoying sister that she would let her meet good old

Stanley. "OK, I'm getting up. Just hold your horses, and I'll be in and out of the shower in fifteen minutes."

As Nicole waited for Taryn to take her shower, she heated a pot of coffee for both of them. Soon, the wonderful aroma of Folger's wafted throughout the house, waking up Johnny from his sleep.

"Um, that coffee's smelling mighty good out there. I think I might have to get myself a cup." Johnny jumped to his feet and headed quickly out his bedroom door. "Which one of you ass monkeys is cooking coffee? Pour me a cup, and make it snappy!" Johnny said with a silly smile on his face.

It was too early in the morning for Nicole to deal with her father's stupid jokes, and she had to make him aware of that. "Shut your fucking mouth, old man! It's not even ready yet! Maybe you should run out and get some doughnuts while we're waiting! This ain't no free fucking ride!"

Johnny couldn't believe his daughter was being so difficult with him, but he didn't want to anger her any more because he was still craving that coffee. "Fine! You win! I'm headed to the store right now to get some doughnuts. Don't go anywhere because I'm coming right back!" Johnny was so mad that he had to do something that his daughter had insisted. With all the anger running through him, he stormed out the front door and slammed it shut. "I haven't even been out of the house since we've been here. I don't even know what's open!" Johnny grumbled to himself, but he paid no more attention as he got into his car and quickly drove away.

"It's about time that son of bitch left," Nicole said to herself. "I hope he doesn't find his way back." After a few minutes had passed, the coffee was almost made, and Nicole could hear the sound of the shower shutting off, so she knew Taryn was finished washing up.

It didn't take long for Taryn to get dressed and ready for the day, and before Nicole knew it, the bathroom door swung open, and out she came.

"Oh yeah! Feeling fresh and clean! Now, where is that coffee—and that fatty joint?" Taryn asked.

"Don't I always keep my word, darling sister?" Nicole replied as she set a hot cup of coffee on the table for her and lit a joint in her mouth.

Just the thought of Nicole thinking that she had been an honest person most of her life made Taryn want to laugh and cry. "I don't know about that, Nicole! Most of the time, you're just a lying little bitch who couldn't keep her word if her life depended on it."

Taryn's words didn't offend Nicole because she knew it was true. "You must understand something about me, Taryn. I'm a self-made woman who takes the shortcuts in life, and if I have ever lied to you, it was probably just to protect you from the truth, which does not concern you."

Taryn had no idea what Nicole was talking about, and she did not want to dig too deeply into it. "Oh boy! Look at the time! It's almost ten o'clock. We should get going. Come on—bring your coffee mug. We'll take it to go," Taryn directed as she began to rush and push Nicole out the front door.

"Now, hold on just a second! Shouldn't we wait for Dad? I just sent him to the store to get doughnuts for the coffee. After all, he's got the car, and we wouldn't have to walk there."

Even though Nicole had a good point, Taryn thought it would be best to just leave in a hurry. "Fuck him! I'm trying not to deal with Dad right now because he's just going to stick his nose in our business, asking us where we are going and shit! Besides, it's not that far, and we could use a little exercise."

Nicole knew there was no way in hell she could persuade Taryn to do the right thing at that moment because she was already so eager to go. "All right, you win. Let's get the fuck out of here. If you don't want to wait for the old man to get home so we can use the car, then that's just fine with me! I wanted to roll up to your stupid lover's house with a little style, but now we will look like two moochers who staggered off a refugee boat—un-fucking-believable!"

Nicole's continuous complaining was starting to get on Taryn's last nerve. "Shut the fuck up, Nicole! You're the one who wanted to go, remember? I didn't want to bring you in the first place because I know you will act so fucking needy and bitchy about everything. Now shut up! I'm already nervous enough. I didn't make a good first impression when meeting his family last time, so I'm going to try my best to make up for it this time. You'd better not mess this up for me!"

After Taryn raised her voice so angrily, Nicole didn't say a word. She knew she was driving her sister completely nuts and thought it would be best if she just kept quiet for the rest of the way there. As they took the last sips of coffee from their mugs, they realized they had arrived.

"This is it! This is Stanley's house. Come on—let's see if he's home!" Taryn said as she threw her coffee mug in the middle of the street and rushed up the front porch steps to knock on the front door. "Stanley! Are you in there?" Taryn couldn't hear anybody inside the house, so she yelled out again. "Stanley! I have my sister here with me, and I would like you to meet her! I sure would like you to come out!"

Nicole began to think that maybe nobody was home. "Are you sure that anybody's even home, Taryn? I don't see anybody in there."

Taryn refused to believe that Stanley wasn't home, and she would do anything at that very moment to prove it. "That motherfucker is here. I know he's here. He wouldn't have anything better to do or anybody else to hang out with! Nicole, we will walk in uninvited and find him ourselves!"

Nicole knew that was a bad idea and did not want anything to do with it. "Stop fooling around, Taryn. We can't do that! Let's just go and come back later when somebody is home."

Still, Taryn refused to leave without knowing for sure. "If that's the way you feel about it, you can stay out here and keep watch, and make sure nobody comes. If they do, just yell out."

Nicole didn't feel like arguing anymore. She knew there was no way to make Taryn change her mind about walking into Stanley's home uninvited. She just held her tongue and waited peacefully on the porch steps while Taryn walked inside and snooped around.

"I'll be a minute—you remember what I told you? If you see anybody pulling up the driveway, yell out! Did you get that? I hope I can count on you. I know I didn't just bring you for nothing."

Nicole regretted coming along and wished she would have just stayed home and masturbated in her bed. "Oh my God, OK. Just hurry up before somebody does come home! I'm not going to jail for your ass! Walking into somebody's house without being invited is just as bad as breaking in."

Taryn couldn't believe how difficult Nicole was being after all the shit she had put up with over the years. "Since when the fuck did you care about breaking the law a little bit? You have been a little bratty-ass troublemaker ever since the day you popped out of mom's fat ass! And you know it too, bitch! Don't give me any of your goody-two-shoes crap! You're a fucking menace and a cheap, pesky slut who suffers from bipolar and addiction to heroin! You are not a perfect child. You are a mistake that fell out of mom's ass, and we just had no other choice but to deal with you."

After everything that Taryn said, Nicole smiled and laughed about it as she stood watch outside, waiting for her sister, Taryn, to return.

The house was almost tranquil as Taryn began to stroll around the living room. The only sounds she could perceive were the rats inside the walls. But suddenly, her attention was caught by another sound, coming from upstairs—a much different sound than rats digging and scratching inside the walls. It was more like a wet and squeaky sound going back and forth, back and forth. Taryn was dying to know what that was because it sounded so familiar, as if she had been around that sound her whole life. Without any thought in her mind, she hurried up the stairs to see what she could discover.

"Hello! Is anybody home? Stanley, is that you?" she yelled. The noise continued to get louder and louder as she reached the top of the stairs. And then she discovered a little more than just a silly sound. She discovered another side of Stanley's family that was very unexpected. The walls were covered in family photos—but not the normal kind of family photos. These photos were more on the dark side of a monkey's ass, which made her want to look to the sky and scream out loud, *Why, God? Why? Why do you create crazy motherfuckers like this?* It was almost too much for Taryn as she slowly strolled through the hallway, gazing at every photo in sight—photos of Stanley taking beatings from his father with an extension cord; photos of his mother eating out the mail lady on the front porch, with her uncle watching and jerking off at the same time. They even had a family photo of them all together at the zoo, with Stanley standing there crying because he shit his pants; his family was behind him, pointing and laughing.

"Man, poor guy," Taryn muttered, but she continued to stroll down the hall. There were three rooms on the second floor—one on the left, one on the right, and one straight down the middle, exactly where that funny, familiar noise that she heard was coming from. "Stanley, are you in there?" Taryn called out, but still there was no answer.

The noise grew louder as she got closer to the last door down the hall. She debated whether she should knock on the door like a normal human being or barge in like an unwanted person. Taryn made a quick decision; she took a short step back to give herself some room to get ready to kick the door in as fast as possible. "Cock-a-doodle-doo! Wake up, bitch. It's motherfucking morning!" she shouted as she kicked the door open wide, trying her best to surprise whoever was behind the door making all that noise. She only found Stanley, lying in his bed, jerking off to a *Little House on the Prairie* magazine.

"Oh, Mary Ingalls! Ain't I so glad that you are blind so you can't see my ugly face. But I'm not—and you sure are pretty, like a coyote on an Amish farm." Stanley was so deep into his favorite jerk-off magazine that he didn't even hear Taryn kicking in the door.

But he sure did hear the sound of her voice when she screamed into his ear. "Stanley! What the fuck are you doing, boy?"

"What the fuck, man? How did you get up here? Who let you in? Trust me, Taryn, it's not what it looks like. I'm being honest with you right now! I was just looking over some notes for a Sunday school project." Stanley was so embarrassed that he almost cried.

Taryn couldn't help but notice how stupid he looked, trying to play it off as if nothing had happened. "Oh, shut the fuck up, Stanley! I don't care if you masturbate. Every grown-ass man out there masturbates at least three times a day. Trust me, I know. I've fucked many weird men in my life, and I don't regret any one of them."

Right away, Stanley felt a little relief. "Wow! Three times a day, you say? I guess I might be a normal human being, if that's the truth. Still, what the hell are you doing here?"

"I knocked on the door and hollered several times, but nobody came to the door, so I just decided to welcome myself in. I hope you don't mind."

It seemed a little strange to Stanley that someone as pretty as Taryn would be back so soon, just to hang out with him, but he didn't make a big deal out of it because he had no friends anyway—at least, nobody he would call real friends.

"So, Stanley, what are you up to today? Do you want to come outside and hang out with my sister and me? We are still new here in Skank Hill and sure would appreciate it if someone strong like you would show us around town."

Stanley couldn't believe that two girls wanted to hang out with him. He felt it must be his lucky day, and he sure wasn't going to pass it up. "Hell yes, I can do that! But we should probably leave now before my family returns. I don't want us to be here when they get back."

Taryn was excited that Stanley agreed to take them around town. "Well, then, OK. That settles it; we are all going on a little field trip. Nicole! Bring your ass up here and meet Stanley. He wants to meet you!"

"Hold on now, you guys," Stanley said. "Remember that my family will be back at any time, so we should probably not stay too long. I mean, we should just go right fucking now."

Taryn paid no attention to Stanley's concerns. She felt that he was being paranoid and needed to relax. "Oh, stop it, Stanley. We're only going to be a minute, and then we're out of here." Taryn continued to wave her sister up the stairs. "That's right, just come up the stairs."

At her first sight of Stanley, Nicole didn't know what to think—except that he was strange-looking, and she wondered why Taryn would want anything to do with him. But she didn't say anything at that moment. She just shrugged her shoulders and asked stupid questions. "So, are you guys the broke-ass family who couldn't pay your rent so you had to move into this shithole? Our family lives in your former house now, and it will take forever for us to clean it up. Thanks a lot, assholes. I wish you guys could have had some damn courtesy to clean up after yourselves. Just saying, just saying."

Taryn couldn't believe how badly Nicole was embarrassing her. "Stop it, you!" Taryn said furiously. "This is no time for you to act like a fool in somebody else's house! Show respect."

Nicole was hard to tame, just like always. "Why does your room smell like somebody's been masturbating, Stanley? It's exactly how my room smells. I bet I got stuck with your old room—damn, Stanley! You sure like to jerk off a lot. I'm going to have to bleach my fucking floors just to get that fucking nut smell out of there!"

Once again, Stanley was too scared and speechless to stick up for himself, and Taryn had to rescue him again. "OK, Nicole, he fucking gets it. Now let's get going; we have the whole day ahead of us, and I don't want to lose one more minute by just standing around talking shit!"

They finally made their way downstairs and out the front door. It was such a beautiful day to journey the neighborhood, and Stanley knew exactly where he wanted to take them. Even though he wasn't too excited about Nicole tagging along, he still went through with it for the sake and respect of his newest friend Taryn.

CHAPTER 14

Skank Hill Tour

Taryn and Nicole had no idea where Stanley was taking them, but they did not want to ask questions. They wanted to be surprised if there was nothing better to do. Without saying another word or asking ridiculous questions, they decided to let Stanley lead the way.

"OK, ladies, the town of Skank Hill was established sometime in the 1800s, but I don't know exactly what year because I never learned that in school—not because I wasn't listening but because I never went. Ha-ha-ha!" Stanley was trying his best to entertain his new lady friends with a little sense of humor of his own, but they didn't find him too funny.

"Oh my God, Taryn, this guy is a fucking moron, and his jokes are so lame," Nicole whispered.

Taryn wouldn't hear it at that moment. "Look, damn it, just let him show us around town a little bit, OK? Everything is fine; you're fine; everything is fucking fine! Go ahead, Stanley! Don't mind us. Continue to show us the fucking way!"

And so he did, even though he felt they weren't listening. He continued to blabber about the history of Skank Hill. "Moving on to our next town attraction—our famous liquor store, Orange Chicken Opium. They say it was built by an old Chinese man back in the western days. He would sell opium to every drunken hooligan in town or anybody passing through. And right over there is our first elementary school, but it didn't last long because of the Civil War. After that, kids were forced to work in factories."

Taryn was beginning to enjoy Stanley's company and did not want the tour to end. Every time she felt Stanley was coming to the end of his Skank Hill tour, she would stall him with meaningless questions. "Well, of course, they had to work the factories. Many of their fathers probably were killed in the war, and the mothers were left to fend for themselves. I don't know about you, Stanley Barstool, but if I had been a single mother back in those days, I wouldn't want to work any fucking farm or in somebody else's kitchen. I would make the damn kids do everything! What do you think, Stanley? What is your favorite animal, and how much time would you fuck it to sleep every night?"

Stanley sure did love Taryn's weird sense of humor, and just like Taryn, he didn't want the day to end either. "Oh boy, Taryn! That is a pretty tough question, but if I could be any animal, I think it would be a cat because they are very ancient creatures and also the king of the jungle. Speaking of cats, it's now time to move on to our next town attraction, which is Whiskers Stray Cat Shelter. It's so nice to have warmhearted people in this town who care about animals. I heard the owner of this shelter is a boring, sober guy with nothing better to do but take care of dirty, stinking, flea-bitten stray cats. I also heard he's creepy and talks to dead Indians through whacked-out acid trips. Would you guys like to go check it out and meet the owner?"

The girls weren't interested in such a thing at that point. Instead, they thought it would be better to draw his attention elsewhere. "Nah, we don't need to check out that place," Taryn said, "but look over there! What the hell is that place?"

Taryn was always interested in the most unnatural things, but this place was a real eye-catcher. It was decorated with human skulls and dead stuffed possums, hanging around the front door. Miss Deathtrap's was the place's name, and there was no way Taryn would pass up this place, even if she had to beg Stanley to take her in there. "Stanley, do you think it would be all right to take my kid sister and me into that establishment?"

There was a short pause before Stanley could speak because he already knew the history of the place, and it wasn't because the owner always caught him spying on her getting dressed. It was because the place was cursed, and he felt it brought nothing but evil to the town of Skank Hill. "There is no need to go in that place now, you guys. There are a lot better tourist attractions in this town than that! That place is nothing but a damn waste of time. An old Iranian fortune-teller lady runs it from Mexico. Well, at least she said she's a real Iranian. I don't know how true that is. She could just be another damn Mexican. But I'll tell you one thing—she didn't catch me doing anything, no matter what she tells you." Stanley made himself clear that he just wanted something good enough for Taryn—but something about Miss Deathtrap's completely mesmerized Taryn, and she couldn't take no for an answer.

"Stanley ... do you want your dick sucked? I can do it—well, you know, I can make your dick go to a place where it's never been before, but I will need you to help me first, OK?"

Taryn had Stanley's full attention at that moment, and without any more complaining, he rolled his eyes, took a deep breath, and said, "OK, if that's what you want, but don't say I didn't warn you. And remember, no matter what that crazy lady says, I wasn't spying on anything! She's just a nutty old lady who thinks I have the hots for her. Isn't that silly?"

Stanley was nervous as he walked in the front door of Miss Deathtrap's, but that didn't bother him too much because he knew a special reward was waiting for him after it was all said and done. The doorknob was covered in axle grease, and as he slowly walked in, the sleigh bells hanging on the other side of the door alerted Miss Deathtrap right away that she had visitors.

"Can I help you with something?" She stood before them in a long black dress and one cowboy boot on her foot. She was an old lady, just like Stanley had said, no younger than seventy-five years old. "I don't know who you are, young lady, but I do I know this Peeping Tom motherfucker! Are you here to spy on my naked ass again, Stanley? What have I told you about coming around here? I said you weren't welcome anymore because you're a sick little shit who likes spying on old naked lady's ass! Crazy fucking bastard! You'd better watch out for this guy, my daring child. He's fucking creepy! Spying on old naked ladies! What the fuck is the matter with him? But anyway, darling, I didn't mean to sidetrack you. I've just known this piece of shit for some time now, long enough to know that he's not good for you or anybody he touches or even glances at—fucking cocksucker! So, what's your name, and what brings you here today?"

Taryn was speechless at first, but Nicole couldn't stop laughing at Stanley's Peeping Tom shenanigans. "That is so funny, Stanley," Nicole said. "Were you spying on this saggy-boobs lady? She is old enough to be your grandma, Stanley!"

Miss Deathtrap couldn't have agreed more. "That's what I told him, but he just shrugged his shoulders and blew me a kiss."

Stanley knew she was making things up to embarrass him. "Hey, that part never happened! I sure as hell never did that, and that's the damn truth!"

Suddenly, Taryn became very upset with how the other two were mistreating Stanley and decided to immediately overcome her shyness. "OK, you two! I think Stanley gets the point, and I'm sure he's very sorry about his creepy actions, aren't you?"

Stanley didn't say a word; he just stood there quietly, just like he always did.

Miss Deathtrap knew right away that he was guilty, but she didn't say anything because she felt that she had been a bitch to him for long enough. The humiliation he was going through made it easier for her to switch the subject. "Anyway, my darlings, what brings you two beautiful ladies here today? I have never seen you ladies before. Are you tourists of some sort? Or just drifters passing by?"

Taryn knew she had to answer quickly before Nicole opened her big mouth and said something stupid. "We just moved here. Believe it or not, Stanley was kind enough to show us around the whole town."

Miss Deathtrap saw the smile on Taryn's face and felt the suspense in the room from her positive ways, but she couldn't bear to spoil the moment for her and her sister. Without further ado, she continued with her professional offers. "I'm sorry to hear that, but let me say that we have a wonderful store here. I'm almost positive you will find something special for yourself. Indeed, I even do tarot card readings if you'd like. Or perhaps you two are interested in something darker than that? It's quite up to you."

Nicole could hold her voice no longer; her curiosity was hooked after hearing Miss Deathtrap mention that there was something a little more bizarre in store for them. "Gee, Miss Deathtrap, what exactly did you mean when you said you had something darker than that?"

An evil little smile appeared quickly on Miss Deathtrap's face. It would be easier to say that she already had them hooked on something they couldn't handle, but she wasn't going to tell them that. "I'm happy you asked, my darling, because what I have in store is something alarming, against all the deceased resting in holy grounds. What I have opens all doors to welcome any demon into your lovely home. What I have can bring your nightmares to reality and then some."

Nicole was glad that she had met a woman like Miss Deathtrap, and she could not wait to find out exactly what she was talking about. "Oh boy! All that crazy shit you just said is definitely for me! Now, what exactly do you have that can construct such things?"

Slowly, Miss Deathtrap made her way behind the front counter where all her valuables were locked away in a glass case. "Here we are, my darling; I have it for you. This book is called *The Happy Bastard*—it's like the slow version of the devil's bible."

It looked like nothing more than an old, dirty black book that had been run over by a huge truck a few times. It was even covered in dried blood and smelled like a dead animal.

Taryn had no idea what that book was about or used for, but she did not want her kid sister to be involved. "Now, hold on just a minute! We don't need this damn book that conducts such things. Besides, we don't even have any money to buy it."

Miss Deathtrap was an excellent business negotiator, and she refused to let any customers who came into her shop walk out unhappy and dissatisfied. "Money! You don't need any money for this silly book of curses and shame. All you got to do is help an old lady by getting on your knees and softly eating my pussy; it will only take a minute. It won't cost you a thing. You can consider it an even trade. And don't worry—I don't intend to let you leave here feeling angry because after you are done with me, then I'll lick your pussy too. I'm very, very good at eating pussy; I assure you of that."

Miss Deathtrap was starting to remind Taryn of how disgusting Old Man Peter used to be, and she could not believe how perverted the people were in the town of Skank Hill. "I swear all you old folks out here are the same. You guys should be ashamed of yourselves! And I don't consider your little deal such an even trade. I know everything about good trades.

My great-great-grandfather was part of the cavalry, way back in the day. He learned everything about good, honest trading when they used to compromise with the Indians. Even President Andrew Jackson himself got in on it. It was history in the making and to this day, it has never been forgotten. We sure appreciate the help from our wonderful Native Americans."

Stanley wasn't sure if everything Taryn said was factual, so he thought it was necessary to jump in on the action to correct some of her statements. "Uh, I don't think the Indians like to be called Native Americans."

Taryn was in the middle of her conversation with Miss Deathtrap, and she wasn't about to let Stanley come in the middle of that. "Oh, shut the fuck up, Stanley! Nobody here asked for your goddamn opinion, so why don't you make like an innocent rape victim and just hold still and wait till it's over!"

Sometimes, Stanley could never quite understand the true mind, but who really can? And so he just stood there, stupidly, and reminded himself to not ever butt in to Taryn's conversation ever again. "Man! Fuck all that! See if I ever try to help somebody again," he muttered. "I'll just stand here like I always do and not say a fucking thing. I guess sometimes it's just best to mind your own business and not say a word." The art of listening before speaking was something that Stanley had to learn that day.

"OK, Miss Deathtrap," Taryn said, "You say you want your pussy licked; then I have a treat. I have somebody in mind who can fulfill your request, and his name is Stanley Barstool, the best pussy licker in town and the most handsome too!"

Miss Deathtrap rolled her eyes and scoffed loudly, as if she was giving the short end of the stick. "Oh, please! This little piece of shit here couldn't make women get wet, even if he tried. I sure ain't going to let him touch me. You'd better make me a better offer than that, damn it!"

Taryn was so sure that Miss Deathtrap would accept that offer that she had nothing else to bargain with at that moment.

Then her sister stepped up to the plate and was able to square everything away. "OK, Miss Deathtrap, you don't have to worry about Stanley doing the job. Fuck Stanley! I'll do it! I'm the one who wants this fucking book anyway, so I'll do whatever it takes, just as long as you keep your end of the deal."

Miss Deathtrap couldn't have been any happier and immediately told the other two to step outside the shop for a few minutes so she and Nicole could be alone in private.

Even though Nicole was a master at eating out women's pussies, she still felt uncomfortable doing it with a much older lady.

"Well now, since everybody has stepped outside, I think it's about time to get down to business," Miss Deathtrap said. Still, there was no movement from Nicole, and her shy and silent ways were beginning to piss off Miss Deathtrap. "All right now, girl, you'd better get over here and stop being so shy. I'm too old to be chasing you around! This hound dog here is catching no more rabbit! Now get over here and kiss me!"

But Nicole was tired of Miss Deathtrap bossing her around and decided then and there that she would rather see her dead than go through with it. "OK, old lady! Do you want your pussy licked? You got it! Lie on the table, and take off that ugly black dress and that silly cowboy boot. What happened to the other boot anyhow?"

"Oh, don't worry about it, my dear child. I was feeling badly for a fix and needed to desperately sell some shit for some cash."

Even though Miss Deathtrap told her not to worry about her missing boot, Nicole felt curious to ask, "Who the hell would want to buy just one boot in the first place?"

It didn't take long for Miss Deathtrap to answer that question. "Who the hell do you think? It was that damn fucking Stanley! He likes to sniff the inside of women's nasty-ass shoes and masturbate simultaneously. He's a dirty little fucker, isn't he? I'm telling you that fucking Stanley is trouble, and you and your sister need to watch out for him before he starts sniffing the inside of your shoes."

Nicole had no time to laugh at her unusual situation, even though it was the funniest thing she had ever heard. She still strongly felt the urge to kill Miss Deathtrap right then and there, and she was going to do it most awkwardly too. She thought how stupid it was to walk around with just one boot because you have a drug problem—that was a good enough reason to beat Miss Deathtrap down with her only boot, and that's exactly what Nicole did.

"Say good night, bitch," Nicole whispered just before hitting her directly in the eye with the toe of the boot. But that didn't do it, so she continued to hit Miss Deathtrap over and over again, repeatedly, as she tried her best to hold her still and cover her mouth so she could not scream or breathe.

"Get the fuck off me, you crazy bitch!" Miss Deathtrap yelled, but nobody could hear, not even Stanley or Taryn; they were too busy debating who would win the upcoming boxing match between Muhammad Ali and Leon Spinks.

Suddenly, the glass table Miss Deathtrap was lying on slowly creaked as if it wasn't going to hold her any longer. As the glass table started to crack, so did every bone in Miss Deathtrap's back. Nicole could hear it as the old woman caved right through the table. In a matter of seconds, she also saw her neck snap in two, and her body no longer moved. After seeing that she was finally dead, Nicole knew she was spending too much time in the shop. She quickly grabbed *The Happy Bastard* book and then slowly walked out.

"Damn! What took so long?" Stanley asked impatiently.

But Nicole had no time for questions. "Taryn! If you don't want me to rip Stanley's balls off, I suggest you tell him to shut his mouth!"

Taryn realized that something more troubling had gone on in there by how Nicole was acting and how quickly she wanted to flee the shop, but she decided it would be best not to ask any questions.

"Hey, man! What the fuck is her problem?" Stanley asked Taryn.

"Don't you mind her now, Stanley. She's just going through some woman issues and probably needs to wash that old-lady-pussy taste out of her mouth."

Stanley's eyes widened as if he knew exactly what she was talking about. "Oh yeah! I've been there before. She's not going to be able to get that taste out of her mouth for almost a week because that old lady's pussy is nasty! Trust me; I would know!" Deep down inside, Stanley knew he had spoken too quickly because he had already told Taryn that he never did anything sexual with Miss Deathtrap.

Taryn just bit her tongue and pretended that she never heard anything.

As they continued to walk as fast as they could away from the shop, Stanley started to feel awful for introducing them to Miss Deathtrap. He wanted to make it up to them as soon as possible—not just because he felt bad but because he wanted to be closer to Taryn. Hopefully, she would forget everything he'd just said. "Hey, guys! I have an idea. Why don't we go over to my house and check out that book! I don't care anymore about my family embarrassing me in front of company. You two are the coolest friends I have ever had, and you will always be more than welcome at my house!"

Taryn and Nicole didn't feel like going home quite yet, just to hear the old man bitch about skipping out on him on the coffee earlier that morning, so they agreed to hang out with Stanley a little longer.

CHAPTER 15

The Happy Bastard

It wasn't easy for Stanley to go back to the house with his new friends. The thoughts of misery and humiliation ran through his mind continuously, but he would not let that slow him down. Even though Stanley already knew that his whole family was probably watching television together in the living room and were probably all going to clown on him and embarrass him in front of his friends the second he walked in the door, he decided to go through with it—not out of courage or some kind of bravery but out of stupidity. He wasn't going to let his family act crazy like they always did when he brought over company. He wanted to prove to his friends that they were tough bad-asses, and he knew how to put his family in check. Stanley had never attempted that before, though, and he wasn't sure how they would react.

It was all fun and games to Stanley as he continued to talk shit about his family to his new friends. He walked down the street with his head held high and his chest stuck out, but as soon as they arrived at the house, all that changed. That hardheaded, tough-guy mentality was no longer there, and he immediately tried making some kind of sorry-ass excuse for why Taryn and Nicole should leave. "Ah! You know what, you guys? Maybe you should take off and go home. Trust me; you're not going to like my family. They are all fucked up and don't like meeting new people for psychological reasons that I do not know."

Taryn and Nicole could not let Stanley fall back into his fears. They felt it was their destiny to help him overcome his troubles and stand up for himself for the first time in his life.

"Look here, Stanley! You can't be a fucking pussy for the rest of your life," Taryn told him. "You're going to have to stand up to them sooner or later, and if you wait too much longer, it might be too late for you. I would not like to see that happen. So let's all go in there together and get it over with. I know your sister is bad, so I know what to expect from the rest of them. Therefore, Stanley, you don't have to be afraid!"

Stanley knew Taryn was right about everything, and so with her by his side, he was able to find the courage and finally walk into his own house without feeling discouraged. Still, he hoped deep down in his heart that just maybe his family would be asleep—but they weren't. He could tell they were all wide awake and planted in the living room because he immediately heard the same old theme song to their favorite family television show, *Three's Company*.

And so he tried his best to sneak the girls into his bedroom without making a solitary sound. But Stanley should have known better because as soon as he whispered to Taryn and Nicole to follow him quickly to his room, he was suddenly stalled by his father, Sanchez.

"Hey, Stanley, goddamn it! Where the hell have you been? And who the hell are these guys? I don't want these crazy fuckers in my house, so tell them to get out of here!"

The old Stanley would have caved in and told his friends to go home, but Stanley was feeling reborn through the power of God. He made sure that his father would hear every last word that he had to say this time around. "Look here, you fucking big black monkey! Don't you dare cross me today, old man! Or I'll drink all your beer and then send you to the store to recycle the cans and keep the fucking change myself!"

"What the fuck is your problem, Stanley? You'd better quit your fucking drinking, or I'll sock you in the mouth!" Sanchez said loudly.

But that wasn't the end. Stanley's sister, Lacy, decided she wanted a little piece of the action. "Don't mind Stanley, Dad. He's just trying to act cool in front of his friends. But I know something that they don't know about him. Something so embarrassing that they wouldn't even want to hang out with him anymore."

Suddenly, Stanley felt he had made a horrible mistake by standing up to his family. "You shut the fuck up, Lacy! Please! Nobody listen to a fucking word she says. She's nothing but a goddamn liar! And a worthless bitch!"

Stanley must have had it coming to him because his sister, Lacy, began bombing away with all the dirt she had on him. "Let me tell you two dumb bitches about Stanley Barstool. He's a little fucking drunk with nothing going on in his shit-for-nothing life! And on top of that, he's never even been with a woman! He has been a virgin since the day he was born. When we were little, my dad and I would always have to remind Stanley to take a shower. He would always go to school stinking like somebody shit their pants, and the teachers would have to send him home. Remember that, Dad? I also remember when my father used to show up at Stanley's stupid school unexpectedly and then storm into his classroom to pull his pants down in front of all his friends and beat his black monkey ass with his brown leather belt! All the kids would laugh as Stanley cried like a bitch. Discipline was something that boy always needed to learn, and he will probably need it until the day he dies. Has Stanley told you yet how small his dick is? Trust me, dear, once you see how small it is, you will laugh yourself to death and understand that there could be no relationship between him and any woman on the face of the earth."

There was no feeling sorry for Stanley this time. Taryn felt deep inside that it was not her place to do so anymore. It was now Stanley's time to stand up for himself against his horrible, fucked-up sister, who had always dominated him for his whole life.

"Look here, 'Lacy lice!'" Stanley said, "That's right, bitch, I said Lacy lice! All the kids used to call you that when you got sent home from school because you had fucking lice. You remember that, you stupid bitch? You should have taken a bath yourself! It was even funnier when the old man made me and Pauley hold you down so we could shave that big fucking head of yours! Remember that, Lacy?"

Lacy was so embarrassed that she couldn't stand being in the same room with anybody else, so she fled to her bedroom, screaming and crying.

Stanley was amazed at himself, and his friends looked pleased as well.

Then Nicole said, "I could show you a real good time."

Stanley was dumbfounded. "Uh, what does that mean?"

"Oh my God, Stanley! I need to educate your ass! You are so fucking stupid, but I'm not going to argue with you about that right now. I would like to find out more about this book we got from Miss Deathtrap. This book is so old and has so many chapters to choose from. It looks like a book of spells. Do you guys think any of this works?"

Stanley began to read the instructions out loud, sarcastically. "'Take two black candles and place them on each side of a mirror. With a sharp object, draw blood from yourself and smear it on the mirror.' Yeah, OK, that's no problem. I've got two black candles in my closet and some matches to go with it. I'm not sure if I'm going to cut myself—that might be going too far."

Once again, without warning, Nicole struck from behind, but this time, it was for a much better reason. This time, it was to punch Stanley directly in the nose.

"Damn! You crazy bitch! Why the fuck did you do that?"

"Because we need your blood smeared on the mirror for this to work! Now, what else does it say for us to do?"

"It says for us to light the candles and say these words aloud."

"You mean just you, or do we all have to say it?" Nicole asked.

"Man! I don't know! How the fuck am I supposed to know all this shit? Let's just say it all together. That will make everything easier."

With the candles lit and the blood dripping from the mirror, they all begin chanting the words: *Mich matar personen in echt vida und I disfrutar it und niemand weib sobre it.*

The sound of silence quickly came upon them after chanting the first spell, but there was no thrilling spiritual experience, as they all had hoped for. Everything seemed to be normal.

"I told you guys that stupid book is full of shit!" Stanley said angrily. "And you made my nose bleed for no reason! Give me that fucking book, you stupid bitch!" He snatched the book out of Nicole's hand. "My turn! Don't worry; I'll pick something that will fuck shit up, and hopefully, it will work this time. Because if it doesn't, we will take this stupid book back to Miss Deathtrap to beat her ass with it!"

Suddenly, a soft side came over Taryn, and she felt like enough was enough. "OK, guys! No more spells. I think we should just burn it or something. I don't know what it is, but suddenly … something about that book doesn't seem right."

But Stanley desperately insisted, "Look here, damn it! This was you guys' idea. I'll be damned if I let you two go out like that! You helped me overcome my fears, Taryn, and now I will help you with yours. And you, Nicole—if you hadn't acted like such a bitch this entire time, I would have never given two shits about being a man for Taryn. Thank you so much for your generosity."

It was a little strange how Stanley was acting, and Nicole couldn't help but blush at his kind choice of words. "Oh! Why, thank you, Stanley! I'll try my best to be more of a bitch more often."

"Never mind that now. You can do that later, after I fuck your sister. Now let's give this book another whirl so we can raise the roof of this joint! How does that sound?"

Taryn and Nicole had no idea what had come over Stanley, but they liked the transformation. It was like he was a whole new person. "Sounds off the hook, Stanley," Nicole said. "You are the freaky-deekiest person we have ever met."

"Don't mention it. Now, come on! Let's see what we can find in this damn book. Ah, yes! Here is another good one—holy ground necromancy. This one doesn't require candles at all or even cutting yourself. It just instructs us to turn off all the lights and repeat these magical words. Are you two really up for this? Because I'm about to hit the lights and say this crazy shit aloud."

Taryn and Nicole were so eager to continue that they quickly gathered around Stanley to chant the last spell of the night.

"Go ahead, Stanley! Speak the fucking words! And speak the words out loud and proud!" Taryn said joyfully as she quickly switched off the lights.

"To the gods above me, I ask you to release thy soul from thy body and let live internally into the pits of hell. No longer shall they sleep in peace. May the thoughts of all negative energy allow them to raise from the beauty of light and enter into the darkness of this world."

The girls' adrenaline was making them very horny; at the same time, they were very disappointed as they once again sat there and waited in silence for something miraculous to happen.

"Fuck you, Stanley! That spell didn't work either!" Nicole said, laughing.

"Fuck you, bitch! You're the one who thought this shit would work, so why are you busting my balls?"

"Oh, stop whining like a little bitch, Stanley," Nicole said, "It's only dark magic. Besides, it's not about whether we experienced a paranormal demon of some sort or didn't. It's about having a good time and sharing it with others."

Taryn knew that her kid sister was right and had no choice but to take her side. "Amen to that! Hey, dude, Nicole is right! Let's not fight about it. Let's just have a good time. I say we throw a disco party right here in your bedroom Stanley. We will blast some music, and I think Nicole has some heroin in her purse, if you're interested. But you would have to support your needle because she can't risk that shit anymore—you know how it is. Ha-ha! But anyway, Stanley, that's what we should do now. Are you down or what?"

Stanley loved Taryn's excellent idea, especially the heroin idea. There was no way he could turn it down, nor could his body because it was jonesing for more. Even Nicole knew it because she could tell by how his body was shaking. If there is one thing an addict liked, it was having another friend to get high with or steal drugs from. "Everything sounds wonderful, you guys! We could probably use more alcohol, and I only have so many records."

"That's no problem, Stanley. Our father's an alcoholic, and so is yours. We will have to raid their liquor cabinets and see what we can come up with. And don't worry about the music; Nicole and I have plenty of records back at home. Just give us about a half hour, and we will be back in a flash and ready to disco boogie on your monkey ass!"

CHAPTER 16

Disco Fever

That half hour turned into a long hour. Stanley waited outside on the front porch like a hungry Chihuahua, hoping that someone would throw him a bone. For a minute, he thought they were going to stand him up, just like every other woman he'd ever met, but suddenly, right before his eyes, they strolled down the street and right up in his front yard.

"What are you looking at, Stanley?" Nicole said. "Do you want a black eye or something? I see you looking at my tits in my favorite sexy-girl party dress."

Stanley was so excited that they were finally there that he didn't even let Nicole's smart-aleck comment get the best of him. "Oh, get over yourself. I wasn't even looking at you. I was looking at your smoking-hot sister, Taryn! She's the one I want to fuck—I mean, get to know and settle down with. But anyway, come on, you guys. Let's get back up to my room and start this disco party!" Stanley had a huge smile on his face, as if he felt this was going to be the best night of his life.

As they entered the house, they could see Stanley's father, Sanchez, sitting angrily on the couch, glaring at them, with a can of Schlitz beer tightly in his hand. He seemed to be hoping that maybe Stanley would pass one of his new girlfriends his way. "Hi, everybody. I'm Stanley's father, and I have a bigger dick than he does! So if you two bitches want to get with a huge dog, I'll be out here, waiting!"

"No, thank you, Dad. We are fine, OK?"

"I wasn't asking you, dickhead! I was asking them, so shut the fuck up!"

Stanley couldn't believe how his father was acting. It hadn't even been one minute since they got back, and his father was already putting the moves on his new lady friends. Stanley knew he had to watch out for that because his father had come in between him and plenty of women before, which was another reason why Stanley was still a virgin. "Come on, you guys, follow me to my room. I apologize for all my dad's actions tonight. I hope it doesn't take you both out of your sex mood because I was looking forward to a wet and hot threesome."

Taryn completely understood what Stanley was going through and accepted his apology right away. "Oh, Stanley, you don't have to apologize to your father. He's just a drunk and probably won't remember a damn thing tomorrow. Besides, we could sure turn that threesome into a foursome if we threw him into the mix. How do you feel about that?"

"We are not doing that shit! You are out of your fucking mind! I would have to throw myself off a cliff if I should ever attempt something like that! Please tell me you're not serious."

"No, Stanley, I'm not serious, but I would be honored if you want to someday."

Stanley knew right then and there that Taryn was the one and only woman he had been looking for his whole life, but he didn't want to tell her in those exact words because he was scared he would run her off, like he had done many times with other women. So in this matter, he decided it would be best to just remain quiet about it and dive quickly into Taryn and Nicole's record collection. "All right! Let's see what you guys brought for us to listen to. Oh boy! Man alive, I don't believe it. You guys listen to the same kind of music that I listen to. You got the Bee Gees, you got Abba, and you even have some old-school Al Bowlly—he's my favorite, but I don't listen to him too much anymore because I keep having nightmares about my mother hanging herself. Yeah, that's right. I see her blood on every flower, and it drives me wild."

Sparks flew in the air that night for Taryn and Stanley. After hearing about Stanley's nightmares, Taryn was quickly sexually aroused and wanted his dick more than ever. But she would not let Stanley know that because she intended to get him good and drunk first.

Taryn was the type of woman who liked to take complete control over her men, and she always believed that she had to sedate the brain of a man first before she could take control of the body. "Let me tell you something right now, Stanley. The past is the past, and another drunken mother will hang herself tomorrow. So let's forget about yesterday's troubles and stay tuned in to the now because that's where we need to be. Am I right, cool breeze, or am I right?"

A smile came upon Stanley's face as he said, "Yeah, you're right. Let's stop all this drama bullshit and start fucking partying!"

And so they did; after all that was said, the beers popped open, and the joints started rolling. The party was on its way, and everybody was having a good time. Stanley wasn't much of a dancer, but he tried his best as the records kept spinning to his favorite song, "Disco Inferno."

"This party is the best damn party I have ever been to," Stanley said. "I'm glad to spend it with you two, the two sexiest women in the whole fucking world!"

There was much excitement in just one tiny room, and Stanley was glad to be part of it, and so were Taryn and Nicole. It was a party they needed after all the hell they'd gone through with their landlord, Peter.

CHAPTER 17

Blind and Drunk

Only two hours had gone by, and the three were already fucked up. Stanley was still trying to swing Taryn in bed with him with his corny pick-up lines.

Nicole, on the other hand, was puking her brains out in the bathroom down the hall from Stanley's room. "Goddamn, this bathroom stinks like a motherfucker! That dirty fucking Stanley! Why does my sister always have to pick all the scrubby boyfriends? Look at this—their fucking shit paper is in the fucking wastebasket! Oh, man! That nasty shit makes me want to puke up more! I will never let Stanley hear the end of this one! I'm going to ring his motherfucking neck!"

Meanwhile, back in Stanley's room, where he was alone with his beautiful crush, Taryn, his corny pick-up lines were beginning to work. "Oh man, baby! You are so fucking sexy! You remind me of Debbie Harry. I used to have a "Heart of Glass" poster that I would whack off to and even play the record to make it feel like she was here."

"Oh, Stanley, do you think I look like her? She is, like, my idol. I have all her records. I think she is magnificent."

"Yeah, I think she's great too. Now let's have sex! My dick is so hard for you, baby!" But suddenly, just like that, Stanley's luck slid down, like it had many times before. Because for some reason, all the power in the house went out completely, and everybody was in darkness. "What the hell? What the fuck happened?" Stanley shouted angrily. "I can't fucking believe this! Every time I get close to finally getting some pussy, something always has to go down! Hey, Dad! Did you remember to pay the fucking electric bill?"

"We just moved in this house, you stupid son of bitch! Our first bill is not due until sometime next month, so don't you try to put the fucking blame on me!"

It was so dark and nobody in the house could see anything, but Stanley's older brother, Pauley, was able to follow his father, Sanchez's, voice no matter where he went in the house. So without any kind of warning, he quickly dug his hands into his father's ass crack and yelled, "Oh yeah! I like my old men raw, naked, and useless!"

"Hey, motherfucker! Who the hell was that? Stanley, is that you?" Sanchez said.

"No, Dad! It's me, your older son—your gay and horny son!"

"You sick son of a bitch! You'd better keep your hands off my ass, or I'll hunt your little boyfriend down and set him fucking straight, the good old American way!"

"Which way would that be, Dad? That's my man you're talking about," Pauley said.

"Back in my day, son, the only way to set a gay man straight was by taking a belt across his big hairy ass until every speck of hair fell out completely. And then, when all that was said and done, we'd take one pretty female, maybe two, and lock them in a quiet room together for about a week, and when he comes out that room, the thoughts of sucking a good juicy dick would never come to mind ever again. How do you like those apples, Junior?"

"Dear heavens, no. Ryan the polar bear is the only gay guy in Skank Hill, and without him, I have no dick to sit on! And boy, do I need a dick to sit on! So you'd better not say a damn thing to him—you hear me?"

"Yeah, goddamn it, I hear you. Now shut your fucking mouth. I have to figure out why the fucking lights are out. Stanley! Bring your ass out here and help me find that goddamn panel box!"

Stanley was way too drunk to look for a panel box in a pitch-dark house, but he did it anyway. "All right, Taryn, you'd better stay here for a while. This will only be a minute—I hope. I don't know. But I'll be back before you know it. And one more thing—you'd better take some of these candles and light them up if you want to see around here."

"What are you doing with candles in your room, Stanley?"

"My drunken father has put our family in this mess plenty of times before. Most of the time it's because he never paid the fucking electric bill, but he said he did this time."

"Hold on—wait! What about Nicole? She's still in the bathroom. You help your dad find the panel box, and I'll get Nicole. I bet you anything she's passed out. Fucking bitch can never hold her liquor."

So now, with only a few candles lit and no more time to waste, they went their separate ways and promised to meet back in the room in ten minutes. Stanley's father, Sanchez, was more prepared than anybody else because he had the entire living room lit with candles just minutes after Pauley's grabbing-ass incident.

As soon as Stanley stepped into the living room, he realized something significant was changing. He usually would see his own shadow bouncing off the walls when the candles were shining so brightly, but this time there weren't shadows. At the same time, an awful odor came out of nowhere, smelling up the front room really bad.

"Stanley! You stinking bastard! Did you fart? I should smack you for that one, you little shit!"

"It wasn't me, Dad," Stanley said.

"Yeah, right! Who else would it fucking be? And don't try blaming your sister because she's upstairs in her room, sleeping, though probably still pissed off for what you said. After we find the panel box and switch these lights back on, you should take your ass up there and apologize to her."

"Suck my dick, old man. I'm not doing that shit! This is not the laid-back forties anymore! It's the seventies! And in the seventies, nobody gives a fucking shit about nothing! Now, please—let's just find this panel box really quick and both be on our way."

Like always when Stanley and his father argued, Sanchez had to get the last word. "First of all, you little piece of shit, the forties were not laid-back for anybody! It was one of the worst decades for all Americans! You would have never made it in those times, Stanley, because you're a fucking pussy! Just like your whore mother! Maybe you should go dig the bitch up from her grave and crawl up her pussy because that's where pussies hide out—right up their own mother's pussy! Ha-ha-ha!"

Slugging his father across the face came to Stanley's mind immediately, but he just couldn't bear to do it. Stanley knew that moment would one day come, for he knew that his father was just a waste of time and energy.

"I found it! I found the panel box!" Pauley yelled from the kitchen.

As soon as they heard that, Stanley and his father quickly rushed to the kitchen to see if they could resolve the problem. Everything was intact as they held their candles close to the box to get a better look.

"I don't know what the hell is going on here, but there is nothing wrong with the panel box, and we paid the fucking electric bill," Sanchez said.

For a brief moment, Stanley had the idea that just maybe *The Happy Bastard* witchcraft book might have worked. But the alcohol running through him made him think less of it.

Meanwhile, as planned, Taryn needed to rescue her sister's drunk ass from the bathroom, bring her back to the bedroom, and wait for Stanley. As soon as she found the bathroom door in the hallway, she knocked very heavily, and the door swung open instantly. "Nicole? Are you feeling OK?" There were no signs that she was sick as she stood there with a grin on her face, gazing into the mirror above the sink. "What the fuck are you doing, Nicole? Come on; we got to get back to the room and wait for Stanley."

"You go wait for him, bitch! That's your fucking man! I never would dedicate myself to just one man—that is so boring! I'm going to make sure every man in the world knows about me. Whenever my name is brought up or found in the encyclopedia, it will say 'Nicole is the best piece of ass in the whole fucking world.' That's what I want, bitch! I want to be that kind of bitch. I'm going to be one huge, horny whore star! And you, on the other hand, will just be a stupid fucking farm girl, milking cows for a living. Ha-ha!"

It was strange to Taryn how rude Nicole was acting toward her. Her voice didn't even sound like hers, and it was starting to freak out Taryn in a wrong way. "What happened to your voice? Why does your voice sound like that? Stop making your fucking voice sound like that!"

Then suddenly, out of nowhere, all the power in the house switched back on, and they no longer were blinded by the darkness. Unfortunately, another problem occurred. As soon as the lights turned back on, everything in the house was not the way it used to be. It was all completely changed. It changed so much that it made it feel like a different house. The walls were clean and bright, and there were gambling tables everywhere and stacks of hay in every corner. The entire place smelled like cigars, whiskey, and horse shit. There were whores standing all around, smiling and fingering themselves and looking strangely at each other.

Stanley and his father looked at each other and didn't know whether they should run for their lives or kick back and have the time of their lives.

Stanley had a warm heart and cared very much for Taryn; he decided it would be best to find her and her kid sister and get out as soon as possible. "Taryn! Where are you? Grab Nicole, and let's get the fuck out of here! I think that crazy voodoo shit is working!"

"What the fuck are you talking about, Stanley? What fucking voodoo shit?" his father asked.

"Me and the girls—we went out and got this witchcraft book and started setting spells. We were getting drunk, and I was horny. I didn't think it was going to work."

"Oh, don't beat yourself up too hard, Stanley! This must have been a good spell you set—something just for sick, horny fuckers like us! Look around you; there's pussy everywhere! Come on! Let's take a seat and order a drink; it's on me!"

As much as Stanley wanted to stay, he knew, deep down in his heart, that Taryn was the only one for him. He decided to leave his father by himself to drink alone. "Sorry, Dad, but I got to find Taryn and get her out of here. You should leave too."

Sanchez didn't think about Stanley not wanting to have that drink with him. "Yeah, I knew you were a square, Stanley. Go on! Get out of here, boy! You leave all this pussy to me because we know you couldn't handle it anyway."

CHAPTER 18

Time to Leave

As soon as Stanley's father waved him off with his middle finger, Stanley was gone and looking for the love of his life. "Taryn! Where the fuck are you?" He suddenly remembered that she had gone to attend to her sister in the bathroom, but the whole house was so dissimilar from what it used to be that it was hard for him to find her.

He began to open every bedroom door in the house, looking for Taryn. "I'll start with this room first. Taryn! Are you in here?" But there was no Taryn. Instead, he found his brother, Pauley, in a bright red dress covered in glitter, making out with his boyfriend, Ryan, the polar bear. But they weren't just making out; they were also taking turns fucking each other in the ass and enjoying every inch of it.

"Come, Stanley, come join us for a wonderful time. It doesn't feel too comfortable at first, but it's smooth as a baby's ass and tastes like a juicy steak after a while."

Having to witness that made Stanley sick to his stomach, and he could see no longer bear to watch anymore. "You guys look like you have everything under control here, so I'm just going to close this door and be on my way." As soon as he slammed the door shut, he wiped the sweat from his forehead and went to the next room. "Damn! That was some fucked-up shit right now! This is not the time to see what door number two has in store for me," he said softly to himself as he slowly started to walk in to take a peek around the door. "Taryn! Are you in here?"

But once again, there was no Taryn. Instead, there was a lady he hadn't seen for a long time—his dead mother. "You have to leave this place—*now*, Stanley, before it figures out a way to trap you inside!"

Stanley could not believe that his mother was standing before him at that very moment. It was too bad that he was so drunk or he would have taken it more seriously. "Hey, Mom! Check me out! It's me, Stanley! Remember when you told Dad that you wanted to be cremated after you died? He just buried you in the front yard next to the dog. But don't worry—we didn't leave your body at the old house. Nope, sure didn't; the old man made damn sure to take you with us! So now you're buried out in front of this house."

"You must listen to me, Stanley! Leave now! Forget about the family! Forget about that girl! You must leave now, or it will be too late, and you won't be able to escape!"

But Stanley was in love and could not listen to what his mother said. "I can do that, Mom. I'm in love, and this might be the only time I ever get laid. So you best get out of here and go find another house to haunt because this one has already been taken over by many whores."

There was just no way to persuade Stanley at that moment. Not even the ghost of his mother returning from her grave could talk any sense into him. It was hopeless, and so much time had already gone by. "You're going to die in here. Stanley. You're going to die here. Now you tell your father that he's going to die too! And also tell him that I fucked all his friends, and it felt real good, and I sometimes thought of you, Stanley, every time I got fucked in my ass! That's right, Stanley. You have always been Mama's little boy."

Stanley could only take so much. In that instant, he quickly shut the door. "Where the fuck is Taryn?" he muttered. Then he shouted, "Where the fuck are you! Taryn! Can you hear me?"

But still, there was no sign of her, so he continued the search, hoping to find her.

Meanwhile, Sanchez drank whiskey and played. For him, there was nothing to worry about.

"You have no idea who I am, boy?" asked one of the ghosts.

"No, sir, I have never seen a ghost like you before, but I'll tell you one damn thing! You all better start helping to pay rent around here! Dead or not dead, I don't give a fuck! You live under this; you're going to be paying some motherfucking rent, and that's final!"

Sanchez wanted to clarify how everything worked under his rules. Still, some of the odd-looking paranormal succubi were not taking it too well, and neither was the much darker presence that stood before him.

"My name is Sheriff Benson, and I used to run this town a long, long time ago. This whorehouse was the only good thing that came out of this deadbeat town, but it couldn't stay strong and alive because I had to deal with stupid fucks like you! That's how this fucking whorehouse crashed and died. This was going to be the biggest whorehouse ever, but then one day, two stupid fucking drifters like you arrived in this town and fucked it all up. Clayton and Flynn were their names, and they never made it out of here alive. You know what, Sanchez? I don't think you are going to make it out either."

It was already too late for Sanchez. He didn't even have a chance, yet he didn't try to escape. It was like he wanted to be one of them because nothing else was going on in his life. "Go on ahead and kill me. I don't give a fuck! Take that pistol out of your holster, Sheriff, and shoot me with it!" Sanchez yelled.

That idea didn't sit well with Sheriff Benson. He had a much better idea in mind. "I don't think so, boy! Killing you with this pistol would be doing you a favor, and I only waste my bullets on people I care about. And you, Sanchez—I don't care about you because you remind me of every criminal I have ever known! And every criminal in this town will be hanged to their fucking death!"

Sanchez didn't struggle at all. He leaned his head forward and allowed Sheriff Benson and his demon whores to drag him across the room and tie a dirty rope around his neck.

"Goodbye, Sanchez. Nobody will cry for you."

It was done. Sanchez Barstool was dead, hanging by his neck in the middle of the living room, swinging slowly back and forth.

CHAPTER 19
Together Again

Stanley was scared that he might never find Taryn. He had searched almost the entire house but saw no sign of her. Thoughts came to mind that he should get out as fast as possible and leave the others to die. "Damn bitch. Where the fuck are you?" Stanley whispered as a teardrop slowly ran down his cheek. "Fuck it! I'm not going to find her! I need to get out of here before it's too late!"

He began to make his way toward the front door. But just before he walked out, Taryn's voice echoed off the wall right behind him.

"Stanley … Stanley … Stanley …"

"Taryn! Is that you, bitch? Where are you?"

"Right behind you, dumbass! Oh, my God! Where the hell were you? Me and Nicole have been stuck in the bathroom for almost a half hour. I figured you were going to come back to get us! You said ten minutes, remember?"

"Yes, baby, I know, but some strange shit is going on in this place, and we have to get out right away."

"Stanley, what the fuck are you talking about? And what the fuck happened to this house? It seems to be a cleaner environment, and it smells like fresh pussy instead of old-man ass!"

"Listen to me, Taryn! That spell book we used is working! We brought something evil back, and we need to get the hell out of here!"

Taryn didn't know whether to laugh or just slap Stanley's face. At the same time, it was becoming clear why her kid sister, Nicole, was acting so strangely, and it wasn't because she was drunk. But there was no way Taryn would let Stanley know that or anybody else. If anybody found out that her sister might be possessed, they would probably try to kill her, and Taryn could not let that happen. "We have to find that book, Stanley. That fucking witchcraft book is our only hope. If we cast a spell on this house, then there has to be a way to reverse it, right?"

Stanley didn't have much of an answer; he stood there speechless, wishing they never had attempted this whole thing in the first place. "Well … I was thinking more along the lines of just leaving this town completely and forgetting that this ever happened."

"You mean to leave this mess for somebody else to clean up? And walk out like we had nothing to do with it? Stanley, that is a brilliant idea! I don't feel like finding that stupid spell book anyhow, and I wouldn't even know how to reverse the spell. So yeah, great idea! Let's get the fuck out of here!"

Leaving the haunted whorehouse for somebody else to deal with was the answer, but it was just too bad that the tables turned on them once again, as Stanley's sister, Lacy, came from behind, scaring them half to death.

"Is this what you guys are looking for?" Lacy waved the spell the book in her hand. "Are you guys sure you know how to use this thing? Maybe I should look inside and see what I can find."

"Stay away from that book, Lacy!" Stanley warned her. "It has already fucked shit up around here!"

But Lacy wasn't Lacy anymore. The demons in the whorehouse had gotten to her as well. "Mind your fucking business, Stanley! You have always been the little runt of the family, and nobody cares about you. Did you know, Taryn, that Stanley was born slow? The doctor said he's partially retarded due to our mama using too many drugs, too much alcohol, and gang rape activity. Yeah, that's right, Stanley! Your mama was a victim for her whole life, and because of that, you had to take a lot of dicks to the head while you were still stuck in her womb, especially from strangers that you never met. You see, Taryn, Stanley was already giving head before he was even born, so that makes him the biggest whore in this whole house."

"You'd better shut the fuck up, Lacy, and hand over that book before I punch you right in your fucking mouth!"

"You ain't going to do shit, Stanley. You aren't going anywhere either. This is our home now, and you are a part of it, just like the rest of us. You will never leave. *Vacas are violar me*! *I disfrutar it cada noche*!"

Stanley had no idea what kind of spell she was setting off, but he knew right away that she must be stopped before she fucked things up. "Look here, bitch! I always wanted to kill you, but I never got the chance. I don't even need a knife to do it because I'm just going to strangle you with my own hands and watch your soul slowly drift away." Stanley didn't wait another minute after speaking those words. He went right to work on her and hoped that she would eventually stop breathing as his bare hands began to squeeze tightly around her neck. "Die, bitch! Die!" It was an amazing feeling for Stanley at that moment, realizing that his sister, who had troubled him for his whole life, had finally died. Her body was no longer moving, and she wasn't breathing. "Yeah! That's right, bitch! Who's the fucking man now?"

Taryn, on the other hand, had no time to stand around and watch Stanley jumping for joy, declaring victory. She was freaked out by all that was happening around her and desperately wanted to leave right away. And so that's exactly what she did. She quickly grabbed Nicole, and they both raced out the front door, leaving poor Stanley behind.

"Hold up! Wait for me!" Stanley pleaded, but it was too late for him. The house would not let him leave, no matter how much he tried. The door appeared to be nailed shut, and all the windows in the house were boarded up again, just like they'd found them when they first moved in. "What the fuck is going on here? Taryn! Don't leave me! I love you!" Stanley couldn't believe that, once again, he was so close to finding true love, and just like that, she ran out of his life—and there was nothing he could do about it.

But just when Stanley thought things couldn't get any worse, the voice of his dead sister came creeping from behind. She was still alive.

"What's the matter, Stanley? It looks like your bitch ran off on you again! I told you that you will never get laid, and you will die a fucking virgin because you're a motherfucking loser!"

Stanley felt sick and had nothing left to do but cry. It was the worst day of his life, and he wished deep down inside that it would just end. But luck finally was on his side because he manifested the right thing, and

Sheriff Benson and his new best friends, Clayton and Flynn, appeared right before him.

"Hard times, boy?" the sheriff asked. "I understand hard times. I was living in this country when shit was fucked up. You Americans these days are a bunch of whining fucking babies! But because I feel sorry for you, I'm going to help you out. Sometimes in life, Stanley, desperate times call for desperate measures." Sheriff Benson then smirked at Stanley and slowly removed his Colt Navy revolver from his holster and handed it to Stanley. "Here you are, boy. Go out with a bang, and join the rest of us!"

The situation was hopeless, and Stanley knew it. So now, with all the courage in his soul and with tears running down his cheeks from a broken heart, he finally put the gun to his head, without any hesitation, and pulled the trigger.

CHAPTER 20

Skank Hill Zombies

The second that Taryn and Nicole ran out the front door, they felt relief. The wonderful scent of fresh air and the wind blowing through their hair made it seem like everything would be all right.

But it wasn't. Even though they had escaped from the house, another problem remained: the rise of the Skank Hill dead. Taryn had forgotten all about the second spell they had set off, and now zombies were lurking everywhere.

"Oh fuck, man! What the fuck did we get ourselves into this time? Come on, Nicole, let's go!"

But Nicole didn't want to go quite yet, her mind was still possessed and a little traumatized from the house, and Taryn had to make a resistant decision then and there.

"There is no reason to leave yet, Taryn! These creatures haven't fucked in years, and they're just horny! Let's just stick around and suck their dicks off. I promise you they will return to their graves after that."

"Fine, then! Fucking stay here! I'm leaving! I'm getting out of this town. I'm going home to get Dad, and we are out of here! Goodbye, kid sister. I'll always love you." She quickly gave Nicole one kiss and a hug goodbye and then went on her way to save her father. With time running out, Taryn ran as fast as she could to get home to warn her father. The creatures moved very slowly. It was easy for her to zoom right by them.

The only time Taryn looked back was when she overheard Nicole yelling, "Hey, Taryn, look! Guess who's back from the dead? It's Miss

Deathtrap! Hello, Miss Deathtrap. I thought I killed you, but it seems you are still alive. Stay away, Miss Deathtrap! I'm sorry, OK? Just pull your dress up, and I'll eat your pussy for you. I still you owe you a good pussy licking, remember?"

But it was too late for Nicole. While Nicole was busy, trying her best to keep Miss Deathtrap from eating her, the other creatures slowly crept up from behind and began to eat her alive.

"Ah! Taryn, help! Come back! Ahhh!"

The sound of her sister screaming to her death while being eaten alive by these strange creatures, which she had never seen or dealt with before, made her cry instantly. No matter how much she wanted to go back and save her, she knew it was too risky, and she had to keep going. After that, there was no more looking back. Taryn ran and ran until she finally reached the front door of her house and burst right in, like a police raid.

"Dad! Come on—get up! We have to leave town now! I have no time to explain, but I will later."

"Now, hold on just a minute! We just got here, and there is no way in hell I'm leaving until you tell me what's going on. Did you and Nicole do something crazy again? Aw, man! You guys better not have brought any kind of heat back to this place. We were supposed to leave that crazy lifestyle back at home, and now it seems you brought it with you! And why are you the only one here? Where is your sister?"

"She's dead, Dad. We set off a spell from a witchcraft book, and now the dead have come back alive! They already got her, and now they are on their way here!"

There was no way Johnny believed a word she said; and because of that, Taryn had no other choice but to leave her father behind for a while.

"Oh, get the fuck out of here, Taryn! You have been reading too much *Monster* magazine, and now you are as crazy as a fucking loon!"

"Fine, then! Don't believe me, but I'm leaving, and I'm taking the car too!"

"I don't care what you do. Just make sure to fill the car up with gas this time, you cheap fucking bitch. You and your sister always take the car out and forget to fill it up with gas."

Suddenly, their father-and-daughter argument was interrupted by zombies busting through their windows. Glass flew everywhere, and Taryn ran out the back door as fast as she could, leaving her father behind to die.

"Who the fuck are these guys, Taryn? Hey, now! We don't have anything in this house if you all are looking for drugs, and if we did, I would be doing them," Johnny shouted.

It was too late for him as the zombies slowly made their way through the windows and surrounded him. And now, for the second time, Taryn had to overhear a family member screaming to his death.

"Fuck! I wish we never did any of this! My own family is dead because of me." But Taryn knew this wasn't the right time to play the blame game. Everywhere she looked, corpses were walking around, terrorizing the whole town, and it was up to her to make her daring escape from the city of Skank Hill, all by her lonesome.

CHAPTER 21

Run, Bitch, Run

This was it for Taryn; it was a do-or-die situation. She wanted to take the car and drive off as fast as she could, but there were just too many creatures lurking all around. There was a much better chance for her to make it on foot.

"Fuck this shit! Fuck all you crazy motherfuckers! I am out of here!"

The night was so dark that it was almost impossible for her to see, but she began running as fast as she could down the street, exiting the town of Skank Hill. The fear running through her whole body made her feel like an Olympic track star as she continued to flee down the street.

The escape wasn't easy for her because suddenly, she grew tired and knew she would have to stop to rest a bit. When she stopped, she was thrilled she did because as she was trying to catch her breath, from the corner of her eye she saw a car that was very familiar to her.

"Oh shit! It's Old Man Peter's car! I forgot that I ditched this fucking thing out here on the side of the highway. It's unbelievable that nobody towed this fucking car. Thank you, God. I love you so much."

Taryn was so happy that she jumped for joy and even played with her tits. Having no keys to the car was no problem; she'd grown up in a family where they all learned criminal things, and hot-wiring a vehicle was one of them. Her father taught her very well. The car door was already open, and it only took a minute for her to get the car started.

"All right! Time to get the fuck out of here!"

Taryn peeled out down the highway and cruised happily for a while, but unfortunately, time was not on her side, as another incident occurred for her at the wrong moment.

"What the fuck is that noise? Oh shit! It's a flat fucking tire! Of course, this shit would only be happening to me. I swear, Old Man Peter, you'd better have a spare tire in your trunk, or I'll find your mother and fuck her ass so bad that even your grandmother will feel it."

Taryn had not only forgotten about ditching Old Man Peter's vehicle on the side of the highway, but she had also forgotten that she had stored his body in the trunk, and when she went looking for the spare tire, she saw his body—but now, he wasn't dead. He had come back as another zombie, just like the others. Taryn wasn't on her guard as he grabbed her by the neck and pulled her inside to eat her alive slowly. Her daring effort to leave the town of Skank Hill had almost worked, but it was cut short.

The curse of Skank Hill would remain as it had been for many years. Whoever entered the town of Skank Hill would never leave Skank Hill.

As for Stanley, his soul would be forever trapped inside a haunted whorehouse with his dead family, whom he hated so dearly. But that might be better than being on the outside, where the rest of the townspeople were terrorized by the flesh-eating zombies that lurked in every inch of darkness, killing everybody off, one … by … one.

Printed in the United States
by Baker & Taylor Publisher Services